The Runner

Ian J. Burton

The Runner

Weidenfeld and Nicolson
London

by the same author
Out of Season

Published in Great Britain by
George Weidenfeld and Nicolson Ltd
91 Clapham High Street
London SW4 7TA

ISBN 0 297 77986 9

Set, printed and bound in Great Britain by
Fakenham Press Limited, Fakenham, Norfolk

Acknowledgement

Lyrics to the song 'Hey Joe' by William M. Roberts
reproduced by kind permission of Carlin Music Ltd.
First published by Third Story Music Inc. 1962.

with thanks to Susan

Sunday

11.55 pm

You have to listen. Don't brush my voice aside – this time. Even when I scream my voice remains small in the noise and the clamour in your head. But you must listen. I have lost count of the number of times I have tried to reach you. You travel, across the hours from dawn until long past dusk, yet you come to rest in the same place, in the same bed. I am your subconscious and I must be heard.

This wall between us – not bricks and mortar – this wall is of darkness with your day-time images coming at me, your thoughts, the things you see and do not see. They come – day long, night long, head-long. I receive them. It all pours in through the dark – hunted, refugee, underdeveloped and incomplete. Against this torrent I try to communicate and you run faster through your days.

But then comes the night and the darkness is outside. Night-time pins you to the bed and punches you until you sleep. This is my time. I shoot images under and over and through the wall between us and you sleep-see them, dreaming you call it. I try to tell you –slow down, there's no peace, too much speed, slow down. You ignore me, you run faster. You are the Runner. It must stop. It will stop. Sleep on – for now.

1

Monday

7.05 am

The machines were hunched up beneath shadows in the semi-lit factory and there was silence.

Sally Warren unbuttoned her coat as she walked along the broad gangway which skirted the perimeter of the shop floor. Her cheeks burned from the winter wind and her eyes were watering. She made her way to the post-room brushing aside the tears not knowing if the wind had caused them or the news she had just heard. Stan had told her and his words seemed to be following – thumping her in the back.

The post-room was brightly lit. She stood in the doorway, sagging hopelessly against the door-frame when she saw the size of the mailbag pile on the floor. It was hopeless. The news thumped her again and she entered. It was all hopeless.

There was no escape from the empty, bewildered shock inside her, from the weekend behind her, or the week ahead. This lunatic week. Christmas was a fortnight away, things should ease next week but now it all had to be faced.

She sat down heavily at the table, her gaze fixed on the rack of pigeon-holes rising up from the back of it. Each little box neatly labelled with a department's name or a person's. She stared at Jim Perryman's name, then allowed her head to rest in her hands.

The second hand of the big electric clock on the wall moved on and Monday morning swept silently by.

The figures were done, the full stop at the end said so. His gaze scanned the columns and he shook his head, then signed his name at the bottom, Edgar Broughton, with the air of someone who has rid himself of a problem. He let the fountain pen rest on the desk and leant back in the swivel chair. It creaked in the silence and his eyes remained on the double sheet before him. The final sales projection. Rows of numbers heading across the page, filtered through each column. Running totals, factors, averages – mean, deviation, standard – heading through to the final column: the amount of each item still to be produced and all in one week. Demand was a long way above budget. Edgar sighed, flipping the sheet closed. He tossed it into the OUT tray, Henson's problem now. He glanced at his watch. 7.08 and 49 seconds and 50 seconds and 51. The digital figures throbbed on his wrist, directly into his bloodstream, as if it was minutes and seconds being pumped around his body, but time does not coagulate, it runs, circulating around clock faces. He watched the numbers change a few moments more and the almost invisible split seconds passed by unnoticed. He rubbed his eyes; they felt raw, gritty. Only two hours out of sleep and already tired ... but, he thought decisively, the sales projection is finished. He reached for a new sheet of paper – next problem.

'Coming up to ten past seven now ...', and the voice coming from the transistor chattered back out of focus and the plate of bacon and eggs arrived in front of him. Her arm withdrew from his field of vision. He began to eat without appetite and the radio poured out its noise into the silence between them. The windows of the kitchen glistened condensation and darkness. The wind sounded cold.

Caroline put the kettle on; he did not look up. Her slow, unhurried movements were suggested by the rustle of her housecoat, blue and yellow in the corner of his eye. The row had taken up residence with them for most of the weekend. Hit and run on both sides. It had gone now and left in its place this silence.

The sound of the newspaper falling on the mat and the gathering noise from the kettle now dominated the room. As she passed on her way to the hall, her housecoat parted slightly, enough for him to glimpse her thigh. He finished the bacon, sipped at his tea. She returned, tossed a letter in front of him as she passed by and set the newspaper down on her side of the table. She switched off the kettle and refilled the teapot then sat down and began to read. The transistor reassumed its role.

David Myers, Esq., said the type face on the envelope. When will you be making another payment, asked the finance company inside. He opened his mouth to speak, feeling sure they had paid but the atmosphere between them prevented the words from forming. He discarded the letter and pushed away his plate. He got up, went to

3

the hall, put on his coat and slammed the door behind him. The wind snatched at him as he emerged from the porch; he let it take his thoughts of the row and turned instead to the week he had to face at work.

There was the sound of a heavy sack being dragged along the floor. Sally stood up trying to brush away the tears. Stan, the nightwatchman, came in backwards, tugging at a mailbag. He heaved it around on to the pile.

'Two more of 'em yet. Never did see so many. Not on the Monday of the last week I didn't.' And then he must have noticed the tear streaks on her face. He looked helpless for a moment then went over to her and held her, a fatherly embrace.

'Cry it out, then,' he said quietly. 'Sorry I 'ad to tell yer. Terrible thing. Poor old Jim. Christmas an' all.'

'But he *wasn't* old. It's so unfair!' And the tears came back to her; she couldn't speak.

'Ah, reckon you're right. Come on, sit down love,' he said, guiding her on to the chair. 'Never you mind all this nonsense.' He gestured towards the mailbags. 'I'll make yer some tea, OK?'

She nodded gratefully, managing a smile when he produced a large, white handkerchief. And still the news kept thumping into her. Alone again, she looked hopelessly around, filled with thoughts of Jim and scenes from the almost sleepless weekend behind her. She gazed at the pile of mailbags – orders and letters waiting quietly to be sorted. She took off her coat, deciding to go upstairs to the washroom.

The figures were done but they would not lie quietly in the OUT tray like they were supposed to. Edgar put down the minutes of the last meeting realizing, that despite being half way through them, he hadn't read a word.

Demand is so high. The thought kept returning. Hardly the worry of a sales manager – he countered. They were doing well, nicely above budget. He shrugged. Someone else's problem now. Alan Henson's, he had a week to produce it all. Edgar knew the projection figures were useless, too late; they should have been ready last Wednesday to be of any value. He had meant to prepare them sooner but there just wasn't time. He shrugged again, pushing the minutes away. He decided to have a coffee, despite all the work he still had to do. With the hurried movements of a man running behind time, he went to the door fishing in his pockets for change.

Outside, the long corridor stretched ahead, a procession of doors to his right and windows to his left looking out on to the shop floor spread in half shadows below. He walked briskly but paused a moment when he caught a movement down on the shop floor. It was only the nightwatchman with a tray. He continued along the corridor, his own echoing footsteps following behind.

The coffee machine hummed contentedly to itself as the money clicked into it. He yawned as he waited. There was the sound of footsteps on the stairs leading up from the factory. He stopped yawning and decided not for the first time, that at fifty-two he was too old for the long hours and the rush and the strain of keeping ahead of the pack. But he was still ahead.

'Morning, Sally,' he said cordially as he took the cup from the machine but she walked past him and disappeared into the ladies' washroom. He ignored his own annoyance as she had ignored him.

On the way back down the main corridor he stopped at Henson's door and tried it. It was unlocked. He put his head inside. The office was barely lit by the lights from the staff car-park outside but he could make out the untidy mass of papers on the desk. He pulled the door closed and went on, the coffee cup burning his fingers now but there was a wry smile on his lips.

Just before he reached his office, at the end, he caught sight of the nightwatchman again, this time dragging a mailbag along the passageway. Demand is too high, came the thought before it could be suppressed. He glanced at his watch. It was 7.18.

Alan Henson lay in the darkness, midway between wakefulness and sleep. The alarm had gone off over an hour ago throwing him abruptly out of his dreams and into Monday. There was a conspiracy. The cold wind outside, the rich, velvet, dark of the room, the warmth of his wife lying next to him, the comfort of the bed – they all conspired to keep him there. His resolve was great enough to keep his eyes half open but not to hoist him out of bed. It was a cruel battle. Dreams glimpsed down at him from the ceiling, gone before he could catch them, beckoning him to follow.

One had been of Sally wearing a white flouncy dress, her

movements slow and tranquil like a replay film but everyone round her was travelling in colour blurs, so fast. She was coming towards him – he caught at the dream, it sidestepped away into nothing. But he could put his finger on the source of that one. Last week was it? Where were the days, torn off the calendar on to the scrapheap – was it Wednesday? The week before, maybe? He searched through the days all piled on top of one another for the one when she walked into his office. The phone was ringing. He was in the middle of yet another row with Broughton and the machines were thumping their noise from the factory below directly into the tension headache behind his right eye. She was there, suddenly, delivering the afternoon mail – in complete isolation from the pressure and bruising futility of it all – smiling pleasantly, her face still fresh with the arrival of womanhood. She stopped him in his tracks right there. It was her isolation from it all which had smacked him across the face, rather than her beauty. She was completely innocent, not guilty. . . . But the phone kept on at him and when he picked it up Brian Mann was shooting questions into him and he was being wound up out of a split second's calm as Edgar waited and the machines just kept on running.

He searched for the split second and the dream again but realized that his eyes had closed and he was going down and down into sleep. His face contorted and a groan twisted out of him bitterly.

The time, its implications, the week ahead and the cutting guilt because he had dozed for so long – they all acted in concert now and pulled him violently out of bed, wide eyed and desperate to find his clothes.

Nancy turned over and he saw her face in a grey finger of dawn. His love for her gathered up into another split second of calm but a changing digit on the clock seized the corner of his eye and he continued to dress hurriedly. 7.22.

Edgar walked back down the corridor from Alan Henson's office, the sales projection figures now redated and buried deep in his IN tray. He glanced unnecessarily over his shoulder, just to make absolutely sure no one had seen him.

Neil Telford flung the tracksuit on the bathroom floor and stepped into the warm shower. It hadn't been a very satisfying jog, too early, cold and dark but he wanted to be at work in good time – eight o'clock if possible. Not that there was much to be done in the Advertising Department but there was promotion in the air and he had made a point of getting in an hour before time for several weeks now. Ensuring this sacrifice would not pass unnoticed he occasionally found excuse to phone Brian Mann, the Managing Director, always an early starter.

Neil stepped out of the waterflow a moment and rubbed shampoo into his hair.

Brian was now based on the other side of the city reorganizing the parent company's latest acquisition and, sooner or later, would be appointed as overlord of the two firms. They were all waiting for this. Neil had decided that if anyone was going to step into Brian's shoes, his feet were the only ones that would fit.

He washed off the shampoo vigorously. A managing directorship by the time he was thirty-five – he was thirty-two now – and Brian was just the right kind of boss to have. In his early forties and still keenly ambitious, Brian was ever watchful of the chance to move on and up. He would promote early. Of course this meant competition from Alan Henson but that could be handled. Apart from Alan, there was nothing to beat – Broughton was too old and Myers had no drive.

Neil dried himself quickly, then stood naked in front of the mirror while he used the hair drier, admiring himself. He enjoyed keeping fit, a jog every morning and a couple of visits each week to the club for weight training or a game of squash.

He dressed carefully and decided he could make it for eight if he skipped breakfast. He slammed the door to his flat and ran down the stairs thinking that when he was MD it would probably be necessary to edge Bette, Brian's secretary, out into the cold a little. She also acted as secretary to them all, co-ordinating the work of the office girls beneath her. It was a very unsatisfactory arrangement; it meant that Bette knew everything that was going on – or thought she did. Still, perhaps Brian would take her with him; if need be he would suggest it, once appointed.

The sports car roared throatily in the cold air but he was prevented from driving off by the sight of the postman a little way down the road. He was standing beneath a lamp post sorting a thick wad of letters.

Neil waited, impatient, tapping his fingers on the wheel, unconsciously matching the rhythm of the car clock which ticked softly to

7

itself. It was silly to wait, he told himself, waiting. Jenny wouldn't write to him. Since their last meeting there had been no contact, there wouldn't be. He had tried to help her; she had virtually said, 'Get lost', and he had.

He waited as the postman came towards him at last, revving the engine hard. The postman passed by. Angrily, Neil released the hand brake and slammed the gear lever into first. The car grit-sprayed the other parked cars as it roared off, its rear wheels tweaking over a frost pool. Second, third, fourth. He noted with satisfaction the postman in his mirror, pausing to watch.

It had been stupid to wait. She wouldn't write and if she did it would almost certainly be sent to the office. She could never remember the address of his flat anyway. There might be a letter at work, then. He shook the idea away, irritated because such thoughts had already ruined his weekend.

He kept his mind on the road and the week ahead. He would prepare thoroughly for Friday's meeting. Brian would be chairing it and the rumours were out that an announcement might be made. He pushed the car along and waited for a chance to slip into over-drive.

The car clock was lying, it said 9.30. He adjusted it as he drove. 7.27.

It's another day isn't it? You won't slow down. You and I stand as far apart now as I dare allow. The darkness between us cannot be permitted to grow any wider or deeper. You are the Runner and you're not listening. It is Monday and you've got Friday to run at. You won't get there – unless you listen. Time is running, running out.

I have abandoned now all the work I am meant to do as you sleep, all the sorting and filing, the retaining and erasing. I no longer supervise the work on your body to repair the damage the day has done. You waken feeling as if you have not slept. You may have noticed or you may have ignored that too.

It is morning. The tide has turned against me and you are even less aware of me.

You must sort your thoughts out yourself.

I am going to stop you. For both our sakes I will slow you down before the plug is pulled on us, and the shut down comes, widening the darkness into infinity.

8

I concentrate now on the place which is waiting for you when you come for sleep. I will take you there, this place where all the runners run.

Tonight you will see. Since you won't listen I am going to show *you. You must see.*

The landscape is waiting....

7.30 am

David's car came to a halt next to Edgar's in the car-park. His thoughts would not stop so easily. He ought to go home and talk to Caroline, fill that silence. He sat in the car. The main lights in the factory had not been switched on yet. A dirty, grey smudge of dawn was creeping around its shadow cloak. At eight the machines would start up, spewing out their noise, and it would all pour into Stores and Despatch, his department.

He watched as a couple of grim faced workers went into the factory. He ought to follow; he ought to go home; he wasn't due in until nine. There was time.

He wasn't very good at rows, argument, debate; he avoided them at work, most were pointless, vehicles aimed only at making an impression and not at finding a solution. His rows with Caroline tended to be about his inability to communicate, that along with the other things he was incapable of.

He ought to go home. The heat was draining from the car, the windows misting. He sat perfectly still, gazing into the receding shadows.

How long had it been? Three months or four since their sex life had died? How many times had he failed in the attempt to make love before it became something they didn't do any more?

He couldn't talk about it. It was something he preferred not to think about even and he dwelt on it now only because there was something else he wanted to think about even less.

Caroline had tried to get him to talk but he couldn't, that was the embarrassing thing really and the circle he was now enclosed by was small and vicious. His failures had seen off his confidence, there was no urge for sex, just the constantly gnawing thought that there ought to be, that there was something the matter with him. He felt ashamed. Everyone else around him seemed to be obsessed with it, even Broughton – ten years his senior. Edgar was known to be a womanizer and Neil Telford wore his women like a buttonhole. Sex was everywhere, behind almost every conversation and he couldn't talk about it.

He *needed* to make love to Caroline, or someone, just to prove there was nothing wrong but for no other reason. And the time gap which was widening between them made it more important, more difficult, making the possibility of another failure unbearable. Impasse.

And, crawling up out of the desperation, there had been Saturday. The thought sat on his shoulder like an evil spirit; he tried to shake it off. Quickly he jumped out of the car and slammed the door violently, his movements vaguely tinged with panic. Any thought of Saturday was left shut tight inside the car. He walked briskly across the car-park. He would keep out of the way today, stay in his office.

The mailbag on the top slipped lazily down the pile, spilling letters out across the floor. Sally almost dropped the cup she was holding; it had been empty for several minutes. She was startled to find herself in the post-room, deep in winter – she had been back to the summer before last when Jim had started her at the factory, on the shop floor.

Jim was big and loud and rough with a heart of pure gold and he had always kept an eye on her. He pushed her name forward when the chance came and urged that she be moved to the offices, to get more use from her 'O' levels. He had kept his eye on her even after that. Only on Friday he had told her not to let the increased work-load get her down. The coming week would see it slacken off and during the week after they could all ease off a little before the Christmas shutdown.

The mailbags came into focus and someone walked past the open door but she couldn't see who. It didn't seem possible that Jim was dead. It didn't seem as if it would ever be possible.

She scooped up some letters from the floor and began to sort them slowly, watching her hands work, remote. She skimmed most of them into the big blue plastic bin at her side. When it was full someone would come and wheel it away to the Order Department. It should be full now. The others would be here soon, it was coming

10

up to 7.40. Occasionally her hands moved out to the pigeon-holes in front of her. Broughton, Telford, Myers, Telford again then Henson. She watched her hands work but when they were empty they made no move to collect more. It would have been better to stay at home; she had spent the night wondering whether to or not, watched Sunday slip into Monday, waiting for the alarm. But she had made up her mind to come, there was no use brooding over the weekend. She would be glad when the machines started; they would cover the numb silence.

Her hands scooped more letters and started to move more rapidly as she began to concentrate on catching up. If Angela had her usual Monday sickness bout and phoned to say she wouldn't be in, Bette would need her to be free as early as possible. Her hands hesitated when the name Perryman cropped up, then blurred on. There was nothing except the letters and her hands – everything else was a nightmare.

David paused briefly in the doorway to the post-room. Sally had been gazing away into space; she looked pale and tired, she had been crying. He opened his mouth to speak but no words came and he moved on before she noticed him. He climbed the stairs wearily and walked along the corridor. He unlocked the door to his office. Its cold neatness greeted him. The desk was clear and deeply polished, a perfect, still-life study in order and tidiness. He sat heavily in the swivel chair, not taking his overcoat off, gazing blankly around the room. Brown hessian. Beige carpet. Just like all the other offices, except for Brian Mann's which was slightly grander – but this was the neatest of them all.

He rubbed his eyes, they refocused on the misty landscape on the wall. He had chosen that, at least.

No words for Caroline and none for Sally. They were all swarming round in his head so fast they couldn't be coaxed into speech. He rested his elbows on the desk and rubbed at his eyes again. It seemed so long since he had actually slept properly, peacefully.

He tried to side-step lethargy by going to the filing cabinet and getting the minutes to the last meeting. He placed them on the empty desk, hung up his overcoat and sat down to read while it was still quiet, forcing himself to concentrate. He became absorbed in them for several moments but he was disturbed suddenly by the sound of tyres screaming as Telford's sports car burst into the car-park. He glanced at his watch. In two minutes the machines would run. 7.58.

Neil sauntered along the corridor though it was the last thing he felt like doing. Satisfaction at arriving more than a minute ahead of the self-imposed deadline had quickly subsided when he stopped by the post-room. Sally was being unusually dim; she looked ghastly and neither of the letters he got from her were from Jenny. Sauntering along the corridor was out of step with the way he felt inside. He kicked viciously at the thought that as, apparently, Sally had only just begun to sort, there was still hope.

So, he sauntered nonchalantly, it was always important never to let the image slip. This was the place for images – along this corridor where the chess game was played.

He turned the key and pushed the door with his foot. Inside, the window immediately in front of him gaped open and the cold wind swirled across the room, fluttering over the sea of paper on the floor as it came.

He stood there a moment, then entered. Holding on tight to the anger inside him, he carefully set down his briefcase, took off his car coat and stepped his way gingerly to the telephone. He picked up the receiver, dialled, waited.

'Neil Telford here,' he said coldly. 'You can tell Stan I want him up here before he goes home. With his log book and fast – understand?'

He set the phone down without waiting for a reply, and then went out into the corridor and strolled off towards the coffee machine, whistling a broken tune.

Edgar took the tape along to Bette's office and left it on her desk together with all the letters he had dealt with. She wasn't due to arrive until 8.30. He returned to his own desk feeling pleased. There had only been one tricky letter and he had plans for that.

It had been worthwhile coming in so early. The problem of the sales projection had been solved. He was now up-to-date with the correspondence and he could spend the morning analysing the weekly sales figures and making sure that he was well covered for Friday's meeting, just in case there was any unexpected flak.

He eased back in his chair and glanced at his watch. 8.09. Now

12

that his mind had ceased its calculations and its reasoning for a moment the quiet seemed to have intensified, grown heavier.

Edgar was sorting out the papers on his desk when the two things hit him – the silence and the time. Silence? At 8.09? He went out into the corridor. Below, the shop floor was now brightly lit, the covers had been taken from the machines, a blue plastic bin full of letters was being wheeled along the passageway but this was the only sign of activity. The men and women of the factory were standing around talking – and the machines lay idle.

He checked his watch again, returned to his office and picked up the phone.

'At the third stroke it will be eight, nine and thirty seconds.'

He replaced the receiver. Moving over to the window he looked out across the car-park wondering how this one could be played to best advantage.

Henson's car pulled up next to Telford's and Edgar watched as he ran across the car-park. Back at his desk, he began to sort through the papers once more, looking for the letter he hadn't wanted to deal with. It was from Brian Mann.

'Morning, Bob,' he called to one of the foremen. Alan hurried, a little breathlessly along the passageway, not waiting for a reply or noticing that there wasn't one. He climbed the stairs and went to his office noting that he had forgotten yet again to lock it. He had hardly hung up his coat before Edgar came in. He groaned inwardly.

'Morning Alan,' he said cheerfully. 'Better late than never, eh?'

Alan ignored the remark. 'And a good morning to you, Edgar, and what can I do for you?' he said, just as brightly and with exaggerated courtesy. He sat down but made no gesture for Edgar to do the same.

'Nothing much, as ever, I saw you coming in and thought you might like to deal with this.' He held out a letter. 'It's not sales, you see, more a production matter, I'd say.'

Alan sighed and reached forward to take it. He scanned the sheet disdainfully.

'God, not another batch of visitors, surely? On Wednesday? Must be joking!' He skimmed the sheet on to the desk with a contemptuous wave of his hand. 'I'm not dealing with this, Edgar. I can't quite see how you've managed to interpret it as my problem and not yours

13

and, anyway, it's dated ten days ago. Playing pass the parcel again are we?'

Edgar always managed to stir up the acid in him but, this morning, he seemed unusually buoyant and reluctant to join in. Sarcasm was Edgar's stock-in-trade.

'Well, I'll leave it with you anyway. I happen to know that most of the party will be production people – Brian mentioned it – I would have thought he'd want you to show them around.'

'And that's why it's been on your desk for ten days, is it? Oh go on ...' He waved him away, exasperated. 'If it's pass the parcel time, Dave Myers can have it, he's Despatch. *I'm* not dealing with it. I've got enough on.'

Edgar smiled faintly at the remark then said, 'Yes, good idea. Actually, to set the record straight, I've only had it since Friday, Telford's been sitting on it. And you're quite right, I should reckon you've got plenty to do, judging by the projection figures. What did you think of them, by the way?'

Alan was alerted at first by the continued lack of response from Edgar to the sarcasm and further by his uncharacteristic pleasantness, then his final remark struck home.

'Staggering increase. Splendid really.'

'I've had no figures from you, Edgar. I've been waiting since Wednesday!'

'Let's see, Thursday it was, I think, when I gave them to you.'

'Edgar, I'm still waiting for them.' He felt threatened. He was being wound up for the big one.

'Well, Alan, we all know you've been up against it lately but I gave them to you on Thursday. Sure they're not in your IN tray, perhaps?' He was leafing through the untidy assortment of papers. Alan stood up, his temper ragged and suddenly near breaking point.

'Yes, here they are. Towards the bottom. Not even a covering memo, most unlike me – but I knew you were waiting for them. Dated Thursday, look.'

The double sheet fluttered to the desk; the contemptuous gesture came from Edgar's hand now.

Alan sank slowly back into his chair and his heart just went on sinking. He stared at the figures blindly, desperate to curb his temper. He looked up at Broughton, all the pleasantness had gone from his face. Alan's mind pushed through a read-out: the unlocked

14

door, Broughton at work early. This was his favourite trick. Why everyone locked their doors before leaving – but try proving it.

At last, very quietly, he said, 'If you weren't so bloody incompetent, Broughton, you wouldn't need to pull stunts like this. Piss off out of here.'

'I'm going.' Edgar's jaw was set, his voice acid. 'It's just this word "incompetence" I'd like you to think about.' He looked at his watch. 'You walked in here at precisely nine minutes past eight. We all arrived here before you. Only you, the Production Manager, saw fit to be late. You walked through the factory and didn't even notice. I make it eight-fourteen now and there's *still* not a machine running!'

Broughton left, leaving the door wide open. The silence rushed in. Horrified, like a man sleep-walking, Alan went out and looked at the factory. He ran down the corridor.

The landscape looks fresh, like a photograph in its stillness, spread beneath this hill top. Down there – to the South – a tangled forest, dense and overgrown. There is no daylight there even when the day is victorious in the skies. No daylight just a brown and yellow half light, so strong it seeps out from the forest and colours this land, colours it twilight. The forest stretches all the way back to the South, woven into its own sense of confusion. A stream wanders from its depths, meandering to the East, and the West, but heading North. It zig-zags as if to escape the forest which pursues – with sentinel trees standing alone, copses huddled together – watchfully.

But, eventually, the forest stops – the stream does not; it flows on to the North, passing this solitary hill top before crossing the flat and yellow plain.

There is a sound, drumming up through the earth, coming in across the distance of the forest. The horsemen. Galloping in countless number and full stampede.

They emerge from the darkness, horses and riders, dark themselves as if the blackness of the forest has clung to them, painted them. These are the silhouette riders and they ride for the North. They cross the stream, a dark tide breaking all around this island hill top, then – away, out across the vast emptiness of the plain. The Northern Riders.

The landscape is set – and it runs. Tonight, you will see.

Alan Henson

8.14 am

'What the *hell* is going on?' Alan yelled almost hysterically as he ran across the shop floor. The group of men remained where they were, watching him. Bob a senior foreman, stepped forward as he neared them.

'Don't you know what bloody time it is?'

'Sorry Alan, but it's Jim,' he said, 'he died yesterday. Don't think any of us can believe it. Jim's dead.'

As if from a kick in the stomach, the breath was knocked out of him. In his mind there was immediate acceptance – rejection – acceptance and, interspacing them, shock. The cycle ran itself through so quickly it seemed constant, not moving at all.

'Jim? Don't be silly ... not Jim. We had a pint together Friday evening.'

But their faces said it was true, everyone in the factory was looking.

'Oh no! Come on, Bob, it can't be ...'

'It was Sunday afternoon. Sudden, obviously, he just went. They say it was a heart attack. No one knew he had a heart problem.'

'Jim? You mean *Jim* is dead?' The spaces in the cycle were beginning to lengthen, fractionally, intensifying the shock.

He gazed at their faces grimly. He must look like them too, now. He glanced at his watch but couldn't retain the time he saw and had to look again. 8.16. Having retained the information he didn't know what to do with it. He felt swamped as the news ran riot inside. Connections, implications sprang at him so violently he had no time to see them. All his thoughts of Jim as a person, as a friend opened out slowly yet within a split second.

Jim is dead. The thought coming out of the mêlée was beginning to stick. He opened his mouth, unsure if he would be able to speak.

'I ... yes ... I mean, I understand now ... about the machines, but

16

... the gesture's made now. See what you can do, Bob ... get them running ... soon as possible.'

Bob nodded. 'Sure. Reckon wherever Jim is he'll be doing his nut right now because of the lost time.'

'Thanks. Be down later.'

He walked away, dazed. Turmoil inside him stopping and starting as if driven by an impulse motor. Each time it cut out there was only the throbbing shock, nothing else, until it cut back in. He climbed the stairs.

8.19 am

Alan sat back in the swivel chair. His elbow rested on the arm; his cheek rested on his tightly clenched fist. He followed the spiral of his thoughts – upwards. His relationship with Jim had been far from friendly four years ago when he joined the company. He later learned that Jim was in line for the production manager's job but had been passed over. His practical qualifications were not in question, only his theoretical and administrative ability. Alan had worked hard to get the team-work approach over to him. Jim's technical expertise and experience were vital to the running of the factory. They still were. Mutual respect developed into friendship and they became an excellent team. Often he would temper some of Alan's grander schemes with hard, straight advice.

There was no one stronger than Jim. When the need arose he worked longer and harder than anyone else. He was probably the most popular man in the factory.

The telephone rang; he picked it up and immediately replaced the receiver. There was a pause, it rang, he did the same again.

He and Nancy had often been over to Jim and Pamela's. He had never met their children. They were grown up and lived away. Alan shook his head. How could he be dead? He was only – what? Early fifties, perhaps? So fit and strong. Dead.

He sat forward resting his head in his hands. Slowly, the sales projection figures came into focus beneath him. The figures were like ants on the paper, soldier ants in columns. He dimly began to take in the meaning of the final column. Against each item down the page, the amount he would have to produce – this week.

He sat up, staring at them. In the absence of anything from Broughton he had been using his own estimates based on previous years. These figures were at least fifty per cent up on those.

He found himself laughing. As if this had been the cue – the sound of the machines starting drummed up from the factory. He laughed, again the hysteria, a release from the unbearable tension that was building up inside.

The telephone rang as he put on his overcoat, still laughing. He left it to ring, slamming the door on it. In the corridor he passed Stan, knocking nervously on Neil's door, a book in his hand. He nodded grimly as he went by, his laughter had subsided now, as abruptly as it had begun.

The shop floor noise swallowed him whole as he walked along the passageway. He was aware of the movement and the colours from the corner of his eye but continued to look straight ahead as he walked out, unsure at that moment if he would ever be back.

8.25 am

The semi-automatic process of driving now took all of his concentration as he tackled the dual carriageway. There were only splintered thoughts, broken up.

The spiral, which had taken him up through his relationship with Jim, now took a down turn, a drill twisting into him.

He turned into a side road, abandoning the car when he came to a park. The factory, the car, his thoughts, they were all claustrophobic and he needed to escape them.

The park was deserted, its trees gaunt, the grass giving way here and there to bald patches of mud. The waters of an artificial lake slapped half-heartedly at the concrete shore line. The wind had died away to a stiff breeze and it seemed slightly warmer though he thrust his hands in his pockets against the cold as he walked the shore. The trees on the opposite bank danced crazily in the broken reflection of the lake. He sat on a bench and looked across at them.

His mind cast forward, hooked into Friday and the meeting. An announcement would probably be made to ease the uncertainty and unrest that had rifled through the pack in Brian's absence. Perhaps there would be no announcement, perhaps Brian had set the promotion hare to run simply to keep them on their toes. Alan thought not. It seemed almost inevitable that he would be appointed; he had worked well, at full stretch, for almost a year now.

He looked away from the darkened, winter trees to his left at a black spot bobbing up and down in the distance on the far bank. It was coming towards him.

He and Jim had devised a new production control system which was beginning to bite deep into some of the former inefficiencies. It was a small company, growing but seemingly determined to take all of its past with it. The system, as much Jim's idea as his own, had been a real breakthrough.

If he was appointed he had made up his mind to recommend Jim for his job, his only worry being whether or not Jim would be able to cope with the political manoeuvrings of Broughton and Telford. Then he had realized that, by not joining in, Jim might be able to break the chain, stop feeding the political under-system. Or he might have been cut to ribbons. But Alan doubted it and, with Jim and Bette, he would have the nucleus of an excellent team to work with; would have had.

The black spot in the distance had now formed itself into the shape of a man, jogging along. Alan watched. He must be in his early sixties, dressed in a dark blue tracksuit. His face was set in concentration; his gaze fixed on the ground just a few strides ahead. The man's breath escaped in white clouds like the exhaust fumes of an inefficient car. Alan watched as the man returned to the shape of a small black dot in the other distance.

The slightly swaying trees drew back his attention. He was getting colder but his brain issued no instructions. It would be nice to be a tree, he thought, branches moving with the breeze, roots deep in the ground, unreachable and the whole being reaching upwards for the skies. The sky was a blank grey, unbroken by any variation in colour. But there was still competition, each tree battling to get its share of light, room in which to stretch out those roots, bring in more food, grow still higher. Not so different, he thought.

The image of the figures on the page came back to him, the faces of the men on the shop floor, Jim's face as they laughed over a pint on Friday. They had been digging at one another in a gentle, friendly way at their differences. Alan with his university background, Jim with his roots thrust into much harder soil, just as fertile.

19

Alan sighed, his grief sharpening. Trees aren't so secure, never mind the roots, it's the exposed parts they chop down.

He got up, stiffly. He ought to go back, go home, drive until he ran out of petrol – do something, anything; it was too cold to sit watching the trees.

He wandered back to the car, kicking at a few soggy leaves. There was snow in the sky. In the car, he realized just how much body heat he had lost. He shivered and started the engine.

8.38 am

He realized he didn't know where he was going but there was apparently a direction and a purpose which the car knew about and he did not. He just drove, thoughts still spiralling up and down and through it all, shock, beating down like rain inside him. The car idled along at thirty. He could feel the warmth returning to his body.

He stamped violently on the brake as the man he had watched in the park glanced back over his shoulder and veered across his path, obviously feeling he could make it across the road without breaking his rhythm. Alan stared at him blankly as he ran away, on the opposite pavement now, oblivious. The car behind him hooted impatiently because he had not moved on immediately. Perhaps it would have been better if he had run right over the man, no one need have lost any time then, except the runner.

The car resumed its journey, heading out of the city fringes and into the suburbs.

8.52 am

A large snow-flake drifted on to the windscreen, melting. He looked at the semi that the car was parked outside, cut the engine. A drive, a garage, a small, neat garden painted with faded winter colours. All the curtains were closed. Down the street a car was trying to cough away the cold.

He got out, closed the car door quietly and walked up the driveway, no longer surprised that this was where he was. He rang the bell. There was the sound of movement inside but it seemed a long time before the door was opened. She looked tired and very pale, dark shadows beneath her eyes. A month ago, the last time he and Nancy had come to dinner, her eyes had held a mischievous sparkle, now they were brimming with pain and shock. She was plump in a curvaceous sort of way, a bright and bubbly lady. She smiled faintly.

'Pamela,' he said, quietly. She stepped back and motioned for him to enter.

The lounge was clothed in the half light that filters through drawn curtains. She sat down on the sofa. He sat on its edge taking her right hand and holding it between his. It would be wrong to talk, there was nothing to say and no comfort could be derived from saying it.

The silence was comforting, not awkward or tense. She had probably sat in this room all night, later today people would come and arrangements set in motion. And the inadequate, sincere words of sympathy would be said, skimming over this same silence which would then be taut and laden. There was nothing to say.

The room was quite cold, there appeared to be no heating. Pamela gazed into the empty, open fire-place. There were ashes in the hearth, a coal bucket, wood and paper. On an impulse he let go of her hand, stood up and took off his coat, beginning to clear away the ashes.

It had been a long time since he lit a real fire. He often used to as a boy when the papers had been delivered and there was still that long, luxurious hour and a quarter before he had to leave for school. His mother would be cooking breakfast and at any moment his father would be home from the night shift.

He laid the fire carefully then watched the bright little flame from the match head spread through it. As he left the room with the ashes Pamela looked round at him. He smiled and winked at her in a way which said 'It's OK – go back to your thoughts.' She resumed her vigil.

When he returned with a tray of tea, the fire was flickering hopefully. The paper and most of the wood had gone but the smokeless fuel was alight. Alan set down the tray and added more fuel carefully. He straightened up, turned and was aware that Pamela was coming towards him. She came into his arms, sobbing.

'Oh no, no, no – don't let it happen – don't let it *happen*!' Her voice was distorted by the anguish. He held her close, her head resting on his chest.

'That's it, Pam,' he said quietly, stroking her hair. 'Let it go, let it go, just let go of it.'

The pain and grief in her sobs pulled at his insides as they racked her body. His shirt grew damp with her tears.

'Don't hold it down. Can't keep it inside. Don't try.'

He made no attempt to stop her or ease her pain, nothing could. She cried on and on. For over an hour he held her, his hand resting on her cheek, gently against her face. Slowly her cries lessened and she stopped. He led her to the sofa, sat her down.

'I'll make us some more tea, that pot must be cold now.' He left her, the fire blazing and shadows dancing round the room.

He came back with more tea, this time pouring out for them both. She accepted a cup from him.

'You need sleep,' he said, 'but you're not going to get it – not today.'

She shook her head. 'The children will be here, lunchtime – about. I phoned. Told them.' Her words were broken by the sobs which follow in the wake of tears.

'You'll be putting on a brave face, knowing you. God knows that's tiring. But you'll sleep tonight?'

She nodded. 'I'll try.'

'Good. Love, I'm going to have to go soon. Is there anything I can get you? Will you be all right, alone?'

'No, really. There's the rooms to get ready, for the children. I don't mind being alone – now – only, thanks Alan, I mean, thanks for coming, big help. I know how close you were. He's always talking about you. But – thanks.'

Alan smiled sadly; he took her hand and gave it a gentle squeeze. 'And you must try to eat something, maybe later?' Again she nodded. He let go, got up and put on his coat.

'I'm going back to work now,' he said decisively. 'So you know where to reach me. No, don't see me out. Anything I can do, just call. I'll pop round anyway later in the week.' He paused at her side, hesitated then squatted down.

'Listen Pam,' he said gently, 'next few days, weeks, they're going to be hell, I know, but don't try locking it up inside – not too brave a face – eh? Let it come out – once it's out you can take it back in and it won't turn bitter.'

She smiled briefly and nodded. 'Thanks love,' she said, looking into the fire and clutching the cup in both hands.

He left. Opening the front door he was momentarily blinded by the glare of the snow. The air was thick with a hundred million snow-flakes taking a diagonal line down from a laden sky.

10.32 am

The world was white and hushed as he drove along. His thoughts had slowed almost to a stop when he was with Pamela. Shadows and emotions had left very little room for anything else. Now they were starting up again. A thought train was quietly trying to talk him into going home, he dismissed it. He was needed at work. He knew exactly what he was heading for. The situation wasn't very appealing but he had been through too many crises and this had to be got through, somehow. He just wished he wasn't so tired.

By the time he had parked the car and was trampling across the car-park, his thought speed was up dramatically. He walked into the factory and was blasted by the warm air and the noise. The thought spiral stepped up its pace automatically as he took the stairs, stepped it up to machine speed.

11.04 am

'Hi.' Alan glanced up from the figures he had been engrossed in, he hadn't heard Neil enter. He strolled over to a chair and sat down. Alan went back to comparing his own estimates with Broughton's.

'Not staying long are you, Neil?'

'No, just wondered if you fancy a pub lunch.'

'Lunch?' He sat back a moment, rubbed his neck. 'Hadn't really planned on eating this week, too busy.'

Neil smiled. 'You look rough, mate. Looks as if it was sleep you didn't plan on last week.'

'Cheers. OK maybe I'll have a bite at the Roebuck, but it'll be a quick one. See you around one-ish.'

'Tell you what,' Neil said helpfully, 'if you're in that much of a hurry, why not just dash into the bar and fill your mouth up with sandwiches and things. The chewing and swallowing bit you can do back here.'

Alan laughed, nodding. 'Yes, OK Neil, experience tells me that your first joke of the day is usually the best we can expect, so you can clear off now, whilst you're ahead. I've got enough work to warrant a requisition for a new desk – bigger than yours even, if such things are made. See you at one.'

Neil smiled, getting up, then became more serious.

'Terrible – about Jim Perryman, rough on you.'

Alan nodded allowing the light-hearted mask to slip a little.

'Yes, I went to see his wife earlier. She's pretty broken up, of course.'

Neil's eyebrows arched in surprise.

'Quick off the mark there. Shrewd move, though. Should go down well on the shop floor, you'll need their support. Nice touch, the parental management bit. Anyway, see you.'

Alan hid the effect of his words but continued to stare at the door long after he had gone. Nothing, it seemed, could be allowed to halt the game. This game of strategy and manoeuvre they all seemed so busy with. It sucked each new event into it and the players picked it over and decided how it should be played for maximum advantage.

He went back to the figures and they were still showing an unbelievable 58·6 per cent over budget. It was doubtful if they could push it all through by Friday but they had to or their customers would go elsewhere next Christmas.

He picked up the telephone and began to load the pressure on to the various departments, his tone urgent. He wanted a complete raw materials picture from Purchasing, a check on all work-in-progress and orders waiting to be scheduled from Production Control and an update on the state of the game from Production Planning. There were whines and moans but his tone remained inflexibly urgent. He stopped himself just in time from phoning Jim to see what the chances were of increasing output.

11.16 am

He was turning the question of output over in his mind when Neil came back, this time with some papers in his hand.

'First proofs for the summer campaign,' he said dropping them on the desk. 'Meant to give you them earlier. Let me have your comments as soon as you can.' Neil had turned to go.

'Great. Is that soon enough?' Alan muttered. 'Yes, OK I'll look at them later.' He waved him away not wishing him to stay. As Neil walked out, Sally entered carrying a basket full of letters. Neil caught her by the shoulders and waltzed her round, laughing.

'Oh get off!' she snapped irritably.

'Any for me, gorgeous?'

'I've just delivered yours, Mr Telford,' she said, unsmiling and continued towards Alan's desk. Neil pulled a face behind her back and left.

'Sorry these are late, Mr Henson. There was a flood of mail this morning. I'll have some more later, I expect.'

'Mm. Yes, thanks, Sally,' he said absently, returning to the figures. 'Not to worry, it'll all get done.'

What *were* the chances of increasing output? The question shot through his mind kicking up all sorts of other questions. What could be done in the short term to fill the hole left by Jim? Why were sales so bloody *high*, against all expectations? There was the sound of the door closing. Why was Sally so miserable? Even if he managed to cope would Despatch be able to? David Myers? His thoughts were racing away again, the spiral now creating a whirlpool effect. He could feel the adrenalin surging as he continued to chip away at the seemingly impossible.

11.17 am

Sally closed the door and went on to David Myers's office. He had his back to her. She put the letters on the empty desk and left with the impression he was following her. She moved on quickly towards Edgar Broughton's office.

'Ah, David, just the chap.' She heard Alan Henson's voice. 'Can I see you a moment?' He had been following her. She entered

25

Broughton's office. He looked up, smiling pleasantly, his eyes on her breasts. She concentrated on the papers on his desk, looking for a place to put the letters. As she left she could still feel his eyes on her. Neil was walking by outside. 'Good, there you are. Is that it? Any more post to come?'

'There may be later,' she said flatly. He moved on without saying anything further but looking annoyed.

Once she had enjoyed working here, now she hated it. Since the weekend she hated it and trusted no one. She looked out across the shop floor as she walked along, the basket nearly empty now. The weekend was so long ago and had changed everything. The factory was alive with its usual activity, the bright, gaudy colours cutting across her mood.

Alan Henson was returning from the coffee machine with two cups, taking them into Myers's office. He didn't notice her. She found herself unwilling to trust even him.

11.20 am

'There we are,' he said putting the cups down on the paper Myers was hastily pushing forwards. 'Well Dave, we've got problems. I hope you're up-to-date. How does a sixty per cent increase in production and orders appeal to you – between now and Friday?'

Alan watched first the irritation at being called Dave and then the shock register on his face.

'Sixty per cent! Are you mad?'

'I see,' said Alan, sipping at his coffee. 'I take it you haven't seen the projection either.'

'No. No, I haven't.' He was hesitant, his face still registering surprise.

'Well, that's the shape of things to come. I thought I'd better warn you. I'm aiming to get that kind of increase through to you by Friday evening, Saturday morning latest.'

He was pleased to see the blank look on David's face.

'It's not on, Alan,' he said suddenly. 'Just not possible, I mean, *how* are you going to do it? Even if you managed it – Saturday is too damned late! It gives me no time to pack and despatch the stuff.'

'Mm. Tough one isn't it?' he said without sympathy. He had made

26

many attempts at making an ally of David in the past but they had all failed. David was probably the most repressed man he had ever met, giving the impression that there was a watch spring inside being pulled tighter and tighter. He rarely gave any sign of emotion and this made him difficult to read.

'In any case,' David was saying, 'you don't seem to realize, as far as *we're* concerned Friday is the last deadline. All those orders have to be packed and out of here by then to have any chance of reaching our customers before the GPO's final posting dates.'

'Oh I know all about final posting dates, David; Edgar's salesmen don't seem to but there it is. You'll have to use the private firms – we've got a contract with one of the security outfits haven't we? They deliver to private addresses. Hire some vans, deliver all day Saturday and Sunday if necessary ... I don't know.' He stopped himself in time from seeing the problem from David's point of view. It was all very well to be negative and say it couldn't be done – it was *going* to be done – he was determined of that. If he could push it all through and virtually save the day, promotion would be assured.

'I'll get you a photocopy of the projection, should give you some idea. I'm doing a random sample on the orders later.' He drank the last of his coffee and stood up. 'Just to check the figures, but I wouldn't hold out much hope there if I were you.'

David reached for the empty plastic cup and placed it in the bin. So tidy, so cautious, Alan thought, exasperated. At least he can meet the crisis with a clear desk. Still, he certainly looked worried, perhaps the situation would succeed in speeding him up a little. There were times when being meticulous and thorough was a distinct disadvantage.

He went back to his office briskly. Sally was walking along the corridor. He stopped her.

'Hang on, love,' he said running into his office. The telephone was ringing. He scooped the projection figures up and gave them to her. 'Be an angel, photocopy to Dave Myers, original back to me.' She seemed about to protest. 'Can't stop. Telephone.'

He went back into his office and silenced the nerve jangling voice.

'Henson,' he snapped, sitting down. 'Morning Brian.'

'Hello, Alan, I phoned earlier, actually, but you weren't there. No one seemed to know where you'd gone.'

'No, I had to pop out, something urgent came up.'

'I see. Look I'm bringing a party of visitors down on Wednesday.

Show them how it should be done. Edgar seems to think you've got the details now – anyway that's not important – I'm really after a letter that was sent in the same batch – that doesn't seem to have been acknowledged either. A job for McKenzie, friend of mine, small order, one off, obsolete stock I imagine – may have come to you to run a few off if all the old stock had gone. Ring any bells?'

Alan looked up at the ceiling; he knew the kind of job only too well. When he was Managing Director he was sure he wouldn't use the factory for non-profit making favours.

'No Brian, it doesn't ring any bells, haven't seen it. I'll look into it for you. Thing is – these visitors – I don't think they're a very good idea at this time. As you well know, we've got trouble here.'

'Trouble? What is it – union?'

'No, fortunately, but Jim died over the weekend and of course you can imagine what a sixty per cent increase will do to us.'

'Sixty per cent?'

'Haven't you seen the projection yet, Brian? I only got it this morning, though Broughton thinks otherwise. We're talking in the region of a fifty-nine per cent increase over budgeted sales this week.'

He heard Mann draw breath sharply and was grateful for that. At least he was grasping the situation.

'Is that on? I mean can we do it in the time?'

'I'm working on it, can't give you anything concrete at the moment but I think we might make it – just. I'll get back to you with some hard facts.'

'Yes, and I'd better have a word with Broughton when we're finished, *must* have this information on time. By the way, what was that you said about someone dying?'

'Jim. He died on Sunday. Heart attack.'

'Jim?'

'Jim Perryman our Factory Supervisor, worked with us for twenty-four years.' He wanted to add the word 'remember?' but bit his tongue.

'Oh, *Jim*! Yes of course I know him. Well that's terrible. Leaves you a bit understrength doesn't it?'

'I'm coping. But, you see, Brian, visitors are out of the question. Yes?' Alan crossed his fingers, hopefully.

'Well . . . it's rather important but I'll see what can be done though

28

it might not be possible at this stage. . . . Anyway, get back to me and
I'll see what I can do. Transfer me to Bette now, oh and don't forget
that McKenzie thing.'

With growing frustration Alan transferred the call then slammed
down the receiver.

'Bastard.' He spat the word at the telephone. The visitors would
come. 'Jim? Yes, of course I know Jim,' he mimicked. 'Bastard,' he
muttered again resentfully. The conversation joined the whirlpool
and immediately the anomaly of the projection figures broke back
at him. Why had Brian not yet received them? If they were ready on
Thursday, as Broughton claimed, Brian would have got them via
Friday's van delivery. After speaking to Bette, Brian would probably transfer to Edgar, and it would be useful to hear what Edgar
had to say. He thought a moment then decided to take a stroll down
the corridor.

Sally had just been about to return the figures.

'Your original, Mr Henson.' Then she walked off looking very
downcast.

11.26 am

Edgar was on the phone when he went in and for a moment he
thought he might be too late but he caught the drift of the conversation and realized he was talking to one of the area sales managers.
Edgar motioned him to sit down.

'. . . yes, but we've been all over this and I'm not having it. It
simply isn't a claimable expense and you can tell him from me that if
he tries it on again I'll have to put him on the carpet. Now come on,
old chap, if you aren't capable of getting the message over, I'll just
have to do the job for you.'

He put down the telephone abruptly. Edgar loved an audience.
He smiled blandly at Alan.

'Well, what's your problem, Alan? I see you've managed to coax
the factory into starting the week, so you can't want my help
there . . .'

'It's these figures of yours – I don't believe them.'

'Well now, what seems to be the matter?' He took the sheet from
him. 'Look pretty healthy to me. By the way, have you heard the

latest rumour? Christmas has been cancelled, apparently it doesn't fit in with Production's schedules. It's being shifted to the middle of April by all accounts.'

Alan wasn't drawn by the remark; all he wanted to do was to sit there until the telephone rang.

'Either the figures are wrong or your sales budget was hopelessly undercast.'

It was a neat point and he could see Edgar appreciated it.

'Oh, I'm quite sure the figures are spot on old chap and, as for the budget – well, I set that over a year ago and, quite honestly, you just can't budget for brilliance – can you? No, Alan, I should concern yourself with getting on with it if I were you.'

Neat, it might have been but it was never going to keep the old fox busy for very long. An idea tore from the lip of the whirlpool and was on his lips before he realized.

'You have withdrawn the range, haven't you, Edgar?'

'Withdrawn? Yes I did that early last week, drafted a memo to all salesmen. Our catalogues are out of the retail shops now.' But Edgar was defensive, as if he wasn't absolutely sure. The telephone rang.

'Broughton. Oh, hello. Just going to ring you, actually. Mm. Yes. I've got them here in front of me as a matter of fact. . . . Haven't you? Really? But you should have got them on Friday's van.'

Alan watched him closely. Edgar's hands were shuffling the figures nervously and irrelevantly around the desk and his eyes were active, not resting on anything for more than a split second.

'Yes of course, I'll look into it right away ... Yes, I know ... Mm ... very important. Yes I'm positive they left me on Thursday, Brian. Actually, I can imagine what happened – probably the post-girl didn't put them on the van or something. Wouldn't surprise me, just had a batch of mail from her – most of them aren't even mine. . . . Yes ... wrong time of the month I should think. Anyway, I'll look into it. Still, Production had them on Thursday and that's the really vital thing.' He fixed his eyes on Alan. Alan stared back at him, unflinching. God I bet you wish I wasn't sitting here, he thought.

'Does he? Does he really? Well Brian – this must be looked into. Yes, certainly I'll get back to you. Fine ... I'll be in touch. Neil Telford, yes, I'll transfer you now.'

He transferred the call and replaced the receiver, his eyes lingering resentfully for a second on the shiny plastic. Go on, Alan thought, say it – I did.

He got up, taking the figures. 'Morning Edgar,' he said with a grin.

'Did you tell Brian you hadn't received those figures?'

Alan retained the grin and let that answer.

'Can't stop,' he said breezily. 'Must get on with it.'

'Well *did* you?'

Alan shut the door firmly behind him and could almost hear the silent 'Bastard' hit the woodwork as he did so.

He took a cup of coffee back to his office. The whirlpool had decided to throw a few answers at him.

In the short term Bob would have to take on extra responsibility for the shop floor. Jim had been trying to bring him on. He would have to take a lot on himself but Bob could help.

If he broke down the figures a little further he could work on the possibilities of laying on an extra shift and that should solve the output problem, or at least clarify it.

He reached for another sheet of paper.

11.31 am

Sally walked into the empty washroom. As the door swung shut the sound of the machines receded a little. Earlier she had wanted them to start up to fill the silence. Normally she wouldn't even notice them but today they had drummed and clattered their way into her already overcrowded head, winding up her tension even more.

She went over to the window and opened it, looking out over the deep unbroken snow. It had stopped falling now. The stillness of it all was calming. Everything was buried. In search of peace her thoughts wandered back to the autumn. Things had been different then, she felt safe and less threatened.

She had gone to the seaside with Gary. It was a cloudy, watery sort of day, quite warm and there was the scent of autumn and winter in the air, clean and fresh. They had spent hours just wandering around the old town, hardly speaking. It was a gentle, unhurried day, relaxed and timeless, occasionally bathed in pale October sunshine.

They stopped to speak to an artist. He had just finished a picture with chalks on one of the paving slabs. It was perfect. He had drawn himself, crouching over the slab, drawing a picture. In the picture it was just beginning to rain and the first drops had fallen on to his work – watery fingers of pastel colours blurred and stretched, merging into one another. It was perfect.

Even as they spoke to him a few drops of rain began to fall and his picture became reality. He just smiled philosophically. It was the best day she could remember, just walking slowly and looking at the movement and the colour and the rhythm of it, hardly saying a word.

A shadow had fallen on it all though, later when Gary had tried to get her to make love and she had clung to her virginity – full of sadness and regret even as she did so. She realized that she had misinterpreted Gary's silence. His was a brooding, frustrated quietness. Although they had been going together for six weeks there had been no sex. It scared her. She wanted it to happen but it had to be *right*, as the day had been. Gary's clumsy and urgent attempts had spoiled it. Afterwards he had been indignant, bewildered, hurt and angry. She tried to explain but hadn't made matters much better though they continued to see each other.

She had let it slip once to the girls in the office that she was still a virgin and had paid dearly ever since. Now she wanted to talk to someone about the weekend but no one would understand. They already thought she was funny.

'Better move it, Sal.' She jumped, closing the window quickly as Angela came busying her way into the washroom. 'God you look awful. The dragon is watching out for you.' Angela took up her usual station in front of the mirror, fiddling in her bag for make-up. 'Cheeky cow, always nosing around after someone, especially me.'

Sally made a move to go, not wishing to get caught up in Angela's web of chatter. 'I'd better go. I wanted to see her anyway,' she said decisively.

'Oh, shouldn't worry – she likes you – she won't say anything. Hey! I never got a chance to tell you, did I? I heard her talking on the phone this morning saying something about getting a replacement for her. D'you reckon she's leaving? I wouldn't be shedding any tears if she was. Thinks she owns the place. You'd think it was her money ...'

Angela talked so fast and her voice had a sickly, sweet, affected tone. There was hardly a chance to put a word in.

'... course, she caught me again this morning, only a bit of fun. I'd dropped my nail file or something and was bending over to pick it up when Neil came in and gave me a slap, you know. I was having a laugh with him but old Bette dragon drawers was there all frosty and businesslike. He might have chatted me up if she hadn't spoilt it. Don't you think?'

'I'll have to go,' she managed to get in. 'I think they're tannoying for me,' she lied as she made her escape. The noise of the machines came at her again in the corridor. She framed in her mind what she was going to say to Bette.

11.59 am

He picked up the phone, dialled and listened to the ringing tone; when it was answered, the roar of the factory gushed into his ear.

'Hello, Henson here. Is Bob around? OK, ask him to ring me would you? Thanks.' He was glad to put the receiver down, cut off the noise. He pushed the sheet away – he had worked out roughly how much time they would need to produce the extra amounts and how many shifts.

The whirlpool had stopped temporarily, giving tiredness a chance to gnaw at him. He was waiting now for the answers to come in from the other departments; that probably wouldn't be until after lunch. He tried to relax, couldn't. He put his elbows on the desk and rested his head in his hands as he had earlier but this time was almost overwhelmed by an incredible feeling of heaviness. He closed his eyes and there was just impenetrable blackness.

'Are you all right?' It was Bette's voice but the heaviness would not allow him to sit up as quickly as he would normally have done. It would not be passed off.

'Oh I'm just ...' His words bore all the usual flippancy but he sat up slowly. '... fine.' The word was lead and sank into position against the way he must look.

'Yes. You look it.' She sat down.

He smiled and for a moment saw the woman she tried so hard to

33

conceal as she returned his smile sympathetically. Her hair was tied back, making her look a little severe. She always chose to wear clothes which would not reveal her figure. Sexual attraction would be an easy and effective card for her to play in the game. She was thirty-five perhaps, forty at the most and unmarried.

'You've got it all to do, haven't you, Alan?'

He nodded. Perhaps she had sensed his thoughts; her voice had softened. He continued to look at her, his mind reluctant to stray back in the heavy darkness he now found himself coming clear of. Bette always seemed apart from the game, remote – disinterested or remote control? Apart, too, from the gossip which moved restlessly up and down the corridor, although she had starred in one rumour a year or two back. The story went that she had been seen at a restaurant with one of the area sales managers, but the real centre of the story had been her glamorous appearance which was received with as much surprise and disbelief as her being linked with the sales manager. Looking at her now, though, he could believe it and it might explain the antipathy between her and Edgar, but not the rest of the team.

The spell was broken; her face assumed its more normal, efficient expression as she said, 'I'm sorry to increase the load further, but Sally has given her notice in. I thought you ought to know. I've spent the last twenty minutes trying to talk some sense into her – without much success I'm afraid. Alan, you haven't dismissed Stan, have you?'

'The nightwatchman? No. Why?'

'Well, she's got hold of a story that's going round the factory. They say he's been sacked and there's a lot of strong feeling about it. She says she doesn't want to work here any more. There's more to it than that, I'm sure.'

Alan groaned, livening up. 'We produce more rumours in this place than anything else. It's a village, a bloody eight to five village! I don't know anything about this Stan business. Look, do you mind if I talk to her, I mean, I'm not treading on your toes?'

'No, please do. I'm only interested in keeping her. She's too good to lose.'

Alan nodded agreement, reflecting that anyone else might have quietly let her go rather than admit that they needed some help to keep her.

'Ask her to pop along, would you?'

34

Bette got up. 'Go easy, Alan.'

'On Sally?' he asked, surprised.

'No, on you.'

He grinned. The telephone rang as she left.

'Henson. Ah, Bob. Can you spare a few minutes, in half an hour, say? Fine. See you then. Bye.'

12.08 pm

'Ah, Sally, have a seat.' But she continued to stand at his desk making him feel like a headmaster. She looked drawn and pale. Her hands were by her sides, clenched tight.

'Now, what's the problem?' he said gently.

'I just don't want to work here any more – that's all.'

'I want you to and so does Bette.'

'But you don't want Stan do you? Why sack him? He never harmed anyone. You'll be lucky to have anyone working here. Everyone feels the same.' She was obviously angry and quite close to tears.

'Sally, no one has sacked Stan,' he said firmly. 'He comes under my department and could not be sacked unless by me personally, or with my knowledge. Is this clear? I haven't even seen Stan today.'

The whirlpool contradicted him, threw out the image of Stan knocking on Neil Telford's door when he had walked out.

She looked at him, surprised and perhaps a little frightened by his change in tone. Some of her anger had transferred itself to him. He calmed down.

'Is there any other reason, Sally? I know you're probably just as upset about Jim as I am. He thought a lot of you, but we can't let natural grief cloud our judgement, can we?'

Quite suddenly she was crying, her face buried in her hands. He got up and went round to her. More tears, he thought groaning inwardly. He put his arm round her.

'Now come on Sally, this isn't like you,' he said softly. And it isn't only about Stan and Jim, he thought.

Angela came in suddenly. 'Not now, Angela,' he said waving her away as he guided Sally to a chair. He made a mental note that it was the first Monday Angela had put in an appearance for ages.

35

'Come on, now what is it?'

'You wouldn't understand. I *can't* work here any more.' Her voice was muffled through her hands but the strain was unmistakable, close to desperation.

'No. You're quite right,' he said sitting on the edge of the desk, 'I wouldn't understand. No one would, would they, if it wasn't explained. How could they?'

'Look, I just want to hand in my notice, that's all. I don't want any fuss.'

'Well I do!' he said firmly. He got off the desk and slowly prised her hands from her face.

'Here,' he said, giving her a handkerchief. 'I want a lot of fuss when one of the best girls we have decides to leave. Do you have another job?'

She shook her head.

'Have you *thought* about this?'

'Think, think, think, it's all I've done since Saturday.' The tears had stopped now. 'I'll soon find another place.'

He sat on the edge of the desk again. 'Another job – sure you will, but this isn't just a job, or needn't be, it could be a career. Jim recommended you and I know Bette is very happy at the way you're tackling things, me too. Being a dogsbody is never easy but it is a good way to learn and gain experience. If it was Jim sitting here he'd tell you to walk out, throw it all up, wouldn't he?'

'No, but ...'

'Of course he wouldn't.'

'But it's not that easy....'

'So, let's talk it out. Come on, I've got all the time in the world and I'll sit here until we get somewhere. What happened on Saturday? Row with your boyfriend and now you don't want to work at the same place?' The guess was apparently incorrect.

'I can't talk about it, really, it's very embarrassing. I don't want to leave but ...'

He tried another guess. 'Has someone here been getting a bit fresh?'

Her head dropped immediately and she stared into her lap.

'I see. One of the management team?'

She nodded. The waters were getting deeper and he began to wonder if he should proceed or not. He would let her next answer decide that.

36

'Sally – we're talking as friends now, in strictest confidence, OK? You haven't got mixed up in an affair, have you?'

'Affair?' She looked up suddenly. 'No, nothing like that, nothing at all. I'm not going out with anyone – not since Saturday. My boyfriend stood me up and then . . . *he* . . . gave me a lift. I was mixed up, needed advice. That was all.'

He paused, thinking. He had been sure, almost, that it wasn't an affair. Sally seemed too level-headed for that and – he sensed – maybe a little too naïve. It seemed a contradiction but in Sally's case the two seemed to meet. Even so, he wasn't at all sure if he ought to proceed, but, the girl needed help.

'So what happened was of a sexual nature, without your consent?' He phrased the question carefully. She was twisting the handkerchief round and round in her hand.

'It wasn't rape, not that far. I think I'd have gone to the police. I suppose I'm being silly and stupid. I needed someone to talk to and he came along. I can't talk to anyone here they laugh at me because I don't jump into bed with all and sundry. It kind of excludes me from their conversations.' Her words were coming quickly now. 'Losing Gary – that was the last straw, being stood up. So I accepted the lift and we talked. It wasn't easy but then all of a sudden he was all over me, in mid sentence, pawing and squeezing and all without any warning or encouragement. I just keep hearing his voice in my ear, coaxing and his breath on me. . . . He didn't hit me or anything; I managed to push him away and then I got out of the car and ran. I kept asking myself – *why*? *Why*? Oh I suppose it was nothing really, the girls would laugh, but I was so scared.'

She stopped as if suddenly conscious that she'd said it all. He nodded sadly, pulled out of his concentration by her abrupt silence. He had made up his mind he wasn't going to lose her. She had a basic common sense most girls of her age didn't possess or were unwilling to display in case it led to more work and responsibility. She was very intelligent, obviously under-educated. The shorthand and typing course the company had sent her on had presented her with no difficulty judging from her results. And yet, despite her apparent maturity there was a certain innocence about her, perhaps due to a sheltered upbringing.

Certain as he was that he wasn't going to lose her he wasn't sure what to advise.

'Have you told anyone else about this?' he said quietly.

'No, not even Mum; she'd have made a fuss. There's no one.'

'I don't suppose you're prepared to name the man?'

She shook her head. He was relieved although his natural curiosity had prompted him to run through the rest of the team. Telford? Broughton? Myers? None of them seemed very likely, not even Neil. Edgar had tried to land her in trouble earlier but that was standard practice in his case when his neck was at risk. David had always seemed devoted to Caroline. Neil, perhaps, misreading her? Maybe old Broughton was getting a bit frustrated in his old age. He pushed away the speculation.

'Do you fear any kind of victimization because of this.'

'I suppose so. It's all so silly.'

'No it *isn't*,' he said. 'The only silly part is you wanting to give up a promising career because of it – and you're not going to – are you?'

She smiled briefly then shook her head.

'No.'

'So,' he said, pleased, 'if there is any further trouble over this – you'll come straight to me, understand?'

Again she smiled.

'One thing,' he said, getting off the desk. 'You were wrong you know when you said there's no one to talk to – there's me for one, you can always come to me – but there's Bette, too.'

Sally went to protest but he stopped her, saying, 'Oh I know she's got this image of being brisk and efficient – all that, but people aren't always what they seem, as Saturday surely proved. Knowing Bette she'll be pretty upset with herself because she wasn't able to reach you. She'd also be pretty upset if she knew I was talking like this.' He grinned and Sally did too. 'But I know *I'd* always trust her – with anything.'

Sally nodded, seeming to understand. She looked at the screwed up handkerchief in her hand. Standing up she said, 'I'd better return this when it's washed.' Smiling.

'We'd better get some work done,' he said going back to his desk. 'I know I said I'd got all the time in the world but these figures don't agree. Don't forget – if you need any help ...'

'Thanks Alan, I mean, Mr Henson.' And she left and there was just the noise of the machines and the figures. He looked at his watch; it said 12.15. His eyes ran back through the figures yet again

38

but his mind ran back over the names and through his talk with Sally. It finally zoomed in on Neil Telford and speculated on what he had wanted Stan for. Anger chewed him over. Whatever the reason, Neil had stepped way out of line and seemingly caused unrest on the shop floor. Neil would have to be stopped.

12.16 pm

As she walked back down the corridor Sally felt as if the day had begun again – only Jim's absence, as she looked out over the factory, reminded her that it hadn't.

She went into Bette's office and sat down at the spare desk. There was a long report to be typed and then the second delivery of mail to be sorted. She loaded the paper into the typewriter, straightened it and then just sat looking at it. She didn't feel alone anymore.

The misty image of that autumn day came back into her mind, framed by the sheet of blank paper. This time there were no shadows. Everything was easy and right. As Alan took her in his arms she felt secure and it was right. He would be capable of taking all the gentleness from such a day and re-expressing it in long, slow, romantic lovemaking, then it would be right.

Wrong, wrong, wrong! She pushed the carriage across violently as guilt dissolved the image like the rain on the artist's picture had.

The telephone rang, it was Alan.

'Hello. No, I'm sorry, Bette isn't here at the moment. Yes, I'll ask her to ring you when she gets back. Bye.'

She put down the receiver and was aware that her cheeks were burning. Bette came in.

'How's it going? Ah good, you're doing that report,' she said, sitting down at her desk.

'I'm fine, thanks. Better now. I'm sorry about this morning. I mean ...'

'That's all right, don't worry, we all get them.' Bette smiled reassuringly. 'I hope things are settled now?'

'Yes, thanks, I'm sorry, I ...'

'Don't apologize – I'm glad it's all sorted,' she said crisply.

Sally felt a little uncomfortable. Perhaps Bette had been upset at her refusal to confide in her.

'Oh, I nearly forgot. Could you phone Alan – I mean Mr Henson. He rang a couple of minutes ago.'

A raised eyebrow signified that she had noticed the familiarity but she said nothing and picked up the phone.

12.21 pm

'Hello, Bette, thanks for ringing. I wonder if you could spare me a minute ... Oh, later perhaps? Yes, just before one would be fine. Won't take a minute ... mm, that's right.' He grinned. 'Yet another favour I'm afraid – OK see you later.'

He hadn't taken his hand off the receiver when the telephone rang again.

'Henson. Yes, Edgar ... No, I haven't got the McKenzie letter. Brian asked me to look into it. Yes, I thought you were finding out what happened to the figures. I'd concentrate on that if I were you.' He put the phone down abruptly.

Bob put his head round the door.

'Not too early am I? Only, I'll be going to break soon.'

'No, come in Bob, sit down. Sorry I forgot about your lunch break.'

He cleared some papers away from his desk then sat back.

'Well, we've got trouble. Losing Jim is bad enough but, as you probably know, the orders are still pouring in and we're likely to end the week sixty per cent up on what we're scheduled to produce.'

Bob whistled. Alan noticed a slight reserve in his manner. He put it down to what he always thought of as the 'barrier'. Shop floor and offices. Upstairs, downstairs. He had tried hard to break this down but it was invisible and strong – undetectable mostly, but it always remained. On the shop floor Bob would have been more relaxed and at home. He looked decidedly uncomfortable even when seated.

'Obviously, we're going to be understrength. The news about Jim – it's like losing two, possibly three men, in one go.'

Bob nodded in agreement.

'So, I'd like you to take on some of his work, on a temporary basis, to see us through.'

'Yes, I see.' Bob shifted his position slightly. 'Of course I'm more than willing, on a temporary footing, to take as much on as need be. Reckon with an increase like that, we're going to need all the co-operation we can get....'

'I can't make any promises, of course, but if you do well, and I'm sure you will, it would do your chances no harm at all when we come to look for Jim's replacement.'

Bob rubbed his chin, reflectively.

'Well, that's what I wanted to talk to you about, one of the things anyway. You see, on a temporary basis – fine, but I wouldn't want to be considered for anything permanent.'

'Really?' Alan hadn't expected that reaction, quite the opposite in fact. 'Could I ask why?'

'It's simple really. See, I'm a foreman on a good grade and – with overtime – I can knock up almost as much as Jim but if I *want* to, see? Jim was staff, no matter how many hours 'e put in 'e didn't get overtime, and – most of those hours he *had* to do, no choice.'

Ah, Alan thought, it's a question of money. He was resolved not to be drawn on this one.

'I see.'

'But it's not the money, don't think that. The true reason is that I don't want to end up where Jim is today – not yet I don't.'

'Ah yes, but Bob ...' he protested.

'No, sorry Alan. Look at the hours 'e did, the worry caused and the frustration with you lot changing priorities – like this morning. Yes I know, you can't odds it, can you? Things 'appen, unexpected. But it's the nature of the job, built in, which is why I wouldn't be interested, not for half as much again as Jim got.'

'OK if that's how you feel, Bob ...' But he wasn't going to be stopped.

'Don't forget – Jim isn't the first, nor the last. We've lost someone each and every year for the last six years. Willis in Accounts, Bradford, Production Control, Newman – used to do your job, King from Despatch, Pearson, boss over Sales. They're all *dead*, man! Just keeled over and "gone" and they all copped it with heart trouble or somethin' like it.'

Alan had known most of the men on Bob's list but hadn't realized the monotonous regularity of the toll. It shocked him.

'So, when you think about it you've just got to ask yourself – why? Is it worth it? I mean, what's it for?'

41

'Well, thanks, Bob, for being so frank. I can understand your views, can't say I entirely agree with them but still . . . moving on, all this extra work is probably going to mean two shifts, twelve hours apiece. I'd like to go round the clock from tomorrow. It's short notice, I know. What are the chances do you think?'

'Pretty good, I'd say. There'll be moans, no doubt, but we've done it before. The lads'll be glad of the money for Christmas. Are the unions OK on it?'

'I'm seeing them this afternoon, but I see no problem there. We'll need to get some temporary labour in but we can keep that to a minimum.'

'The women won't work shifts, I doubt.'

'No, but we can take on some part-timers and lay on a twilight shift. Get the lads to work as late as they want tonight, would you?'

Bob nodded.

'Perhaps you could draw up the shifts, tentatively, based on who you think will want to do what.'

'Sure. I'd better get started,' he said getting up.

'Keep it tight, Bob, at least until I've seen the unions. I'll work on the twilight shift and part-timers. We'll go over it all together this afternoon. Thanks Bob.'

'One other thing, Alan – what's the strength on this Stan business? Only, there's a fair bit of feeling downstairs about it. . . .'

'Nothing to worry about there. He hasn't been sacked I can tell you that. I heard the rumour myself. I'll be looking into it, believe me.'

Bob grinned, reassured. He left.

The lunch break siren wailed and Alan realized that the noise of the machines had died away. He also realized that he hadn't any firm idea what was going on regarding Stan but, politically, it would probably be better to tackle Neil about it over lunch. He would have to have a go at him and yet retain his support. He needed Neil as an ally probably more than Neil needed him. His actions certainly pointed to that.

Thoughts began to crowd in on him. He went over to the window, wanting to escape the mass of papers on his desk. There was about an inch of snow. It had stopped falling but now rain was beginning to follow it down and slush was forming. He watched a few of the apprentices snowballing some of the girls on their way to lunch. He felt very remote from their delighted screams. In the distance a tree

42

caught his eye. He had said he hadn't entirely agreed with Bob but his position had forced him to say that. On what grounds could he disagree? None sprang to mind. It was so easy to pile on the pressure – how many men had he seen who had ended up as burned out wrecks in their early forties? But there were survivors, not everyone ended up like that. Of the survivors how many went on to fall in their early fifties or just before retiring? And the age seemed to be coming down too. He learned, after joining the company, that Newman, his predecessor, had been thirty-eight. But what good did it do thinking?

He thought of the jogger in the park, gazing fixedly at the ground just a few strides ahead. It didn't do to think too far ahead, not in this situation, not even as far as this afternoon when the answers would start pouring in, the shifts to arrange, meetings, the telephone ringing and ringing and ringing, stopping him from dwelling on anything.

But it wasn't like that for *everyone* – look at Neil, he seemed to be wandering around for most of the morning. He always seemed to have time. And Myers, his desk had nothing but a shine on it. Edgar felt the pressure as much as he did – he had always sensed that. They were similar in that respect but their outlooks on people and fairness drew the line between them. Perhaps Edgar was more of a survivor. And they were all in the promotion race as much as he was, certainly Neil – despite his nonchalance. 'It's the nature of the job,' Bob was saying to him over again.

Stop thinking, he made himself say, keep on doing. He turned away from the window and was gripped with the urge to clear the scruffy clutter of his desk on to the floor in one violent sweep – make it as tidy as David's.

He sat down calmly. Bette came in.

'So what's this enormous favour you want of me then?' she asked breezily. He smiled.

'Oh nothing much – to someone of your calibre,' he said shuffling a wad of papers into order. 'It's only this lot – needs typing up rather quickly. But not that quickly – three o'clock would be OK. Could you organize it ... *please?*'

She took them from him with an indulgent smile, shaking her head. She rifled through the papers, saying with heavy sarcasm, 'Oh is *this* all? Top copy, no carbon? You can photocopy what you need.'

He nodded.

43

'OK. I'll try and get them to you by four.'

'Three?' he asked hopefully.

'Five!'

'Four will be splendid.' He laughed.

'Lucky I expected something like this. I also expect you'd like a list of part-timers and the twilighters – names? addresses? phone numbers?'

'You're angelic Bette, anyone ever say? How did you know about the extra people?'

She shrugged. 'It's what I'd have done I suppose. Two shifts – eight, possibly twelve hours each and, generally, all hands to the pump.' She went to the door, waved the papers at him.

'I suppose you realize that when Angela sees this lot you won't be getting your Christmas kiss.'

'Is that a promise?' They both laughed as she left.

He picked up the telephone to tell Nancy he'd be working late.

Neil Telford

1.05 pm

'... and I'd like a G and T and a scotch and lemonade.'

The barmaid walked the length of the bar to the furthest gin dispenser she could find and he watched her from the side bar, appraisingly. He had the feeling that's what he was meant to do.

Her legs were a bit thin but the lowish heels didn't help, high heels would probably improve them. He guessed she had a nice bottom; her skirt wasn't nearly tight enough to be certain; it was probably practical – chosen for comfort, like the shoes. Her blouse was right though, tight, pale blue against the navy skirt. No guess-work needed here, she would certainly never fall on her face. Her hair was perfect – raven, long and luxurious.

She moved well too. Her movements showed the almost imperceptible self-consciousness of a woman who knows she's being admired.

'That's it,' he said as she poured the lemonade. No ring on her finger. 'And, as you won't have a drink with me tonight, you'd better have one yourself, now.'

She smiled. It was something in her eyes that didn't fit in with the flirtatious barmaid image she was projecting. She took the money.

'You should try asking.' She gave him a knowing smile. 'Never know what answer you might get.'

Neil made a mental note of that but just smiled back. He picked up the drinks.

'Won't forget the food, will you, love?'

'Hungry then?'

'Sure but I need food too. Give us a shout, all right?' He left her giggling. Alan had grabbed a table in the corner. He made his way across to him.

'Gawd!' he said as he sat down. 'Good to get away from that place for a break, isn't it?'

Alan nodded, reticent. He had been a bit quiet ever since Neil

45

went along to his office and dragged him out to lunch. He sipped at the scotch and waited for it to hit his stomach and outline the route it had taken. When it did he wished he'd made time for breakfast.

'Weird sort of morning, don't think I'd fancy meeting too many like it.'

Alan looked at him directly. He had the disconcerting habit of looking straight through to the back of your head.

'I suppose it has really – what with Jim going and the snow coming. Mind you, it was forecast – the snow I mean.'

Neil was waiting for him to broach whatever it was he wanted to discuss though he was fairly certain he knew what it was about. He was intrigued to see how he would tackle it and had decided not to give him any help.

'How's Nancy? Have a good weekend?'

'Oh she's fine. Didn't see much of her, I worked Saturday and Sunday, in the mornings.'

'Fix you up with a bed there if you like.'

Alan smiled. He seemed to be brightening up a bit, perhaps it was the gin. A strange mistress, alcohol, he never tired of watching its effects on others and measuring its progress in his own system. He enjoyed drinking but kept it in check. There was a massive advantage to be gained in staying sober whilst the others dropped their guard. He had tried it on Brian once but they were both playing the same game, each pretending to be drunk and watching the other.

'Food shouldn't be long,' he said looking over his shoulder at the bar.

'New barmaid.'

'Yes, not bad, eh? About time they brightened this place up.' The conversation was pedestrian. Neil waited.

'Right bust up with Broughton this morning. Bloody snake. He dumped the projection figures on me – dated Thursday. I forgot to lock my door.' Suddenly Alan was talking quickly, fluently, and Neil thought the conversation was going to take off, as it sometimes did with Alan but he sank, just as quickly, back into his shell. His voice slowed and hardened.

'But you can never quite break him down, you know? Just flashes where you think you get through. Ended honours even, I think.'

'Canny old devil, isn't he? You have to admire him.'

'By the way ...'

Here it comes, Neil thought.

46

'If Brian is stupid enough to let a posse of visitors loose on us, d'you think you could show them round, make it all look interesting?'

No, that wasn't it. Neil immediately searched for a way out of it and decided that evasion was the best course; it nearly always was.

'Not too sure what I've got booked for Wednesday, actually. I'll have a look when I get back, give you a ring.'

The barmaid arrived with the food. She handed Alan his Ploughman's Lunch, leaning over and managing to brush the back of Neil's head with one of her breasts. He made exaggerated faces of ecstasy and Alan tried not to laugh.

'It's not supposed to be waitress service so count yourselves lucky,' she said with mock severity. She plonked a plate down in front of him and withdrew.

Alan grinned. 'Reckon that's another scalp for you, mate.'

They ate. He had no appetite despite his empty stomach. The churning frustration because Jenny hadn't written seemed to be hiding in his stomach and resented the intrusion the food was making.

'I sacked Stan this morning.'

This was it. Neil stopped in mid chew. He had bet against the broadside approach.

'Oh really?'

Alan was staring at him calmly.

'Oh yes. Several people told me I had. In fact, several people asked me what was going on. Silly really but I didn't like to come clean and admit that I didn't actually know. What *is* going on Neil?'

He had never seen Alan quite like this; you could *feel* the anger there, somewhere, but you couldn't see it on his face or hear it in his voice. The effect was menacing.

'I'm not too sure I know what we're talking about, precisely.' He fenced.

'Stan. He was summoned to your office.'

'Oh that! That was nothing. I bawled him out that was all. Every sheet of paper on my desk was scattered around. I'd left the window open. There were designs and sketches; they could have been ruined. He should have noticed the window; it's what he's paid for. Should have seen it from the outside, if he'd done his patrols instead of kipping in the lodge....'

'I don't want to know, Neil. But do me a favour in future and leave me to deal with my staff. That's what I'm paid for. The rumour machine got hold of it and before you know it he's been sacked. Stan had gone home, so it just spread and I've got talk of trouble on the shop floor which I need like a third ear at the moment.'

'Sure, sure,' Neil said holding up his hands in surrender. 'Back off tiger, back to your corner and suck the sponge. I throw in the towel. I shouldn't have blown my top.'

The tension eased when Alan smiled. Neil felt like a child who had been put in his place. Normally only Bette managed to make him feel like that and he'd be getting even with her too.

He was a little shaken; Alan had surprised him. There had been something unnerving about the suppressed anger and tension he conveyed without raising his voice or gesticulating. The thought came to him that he would crack wide open before the week was done. He noticed for the first time a vein close to his right eye, standing out.

'So the rumours aren't true then, Alan; you haven't actually got a third ear like they're all saying?'

Alan laughed and the last of the tension was gone from the surface at least. Neil stood up. He couldn't eat any more.

'I'll get some drinks.'

'No, it's my round.'

'It's OK. I want to chat this barmaid up.' He winked and took the glasses.

At the bar, he felt slightly relieved to be away from Alan. Tension, he told himself, is not infectious. He watched her as she worked. The old excitement stirred, faintly. The thrill of the chase. The chase, he had decided, was on. The run of his thoughts reminded him of the chase game they had played at school. Chain tig it was called. As each person was caught he had to join on the chain and go after the others. He was always the last to be caught. The sudden and overwhelming feeling that he had no wish or intention of returning to work swept through him and joined on the empty weekend behind him and – any thought of Jenny.

She plonked two drinks in front of him.

'It was the same again, wasn't it?'

He smiled, hiding the fact that he had been pushed violently out of his thoughts.

'Thanks, my love. Another one yourself?'

'Yes, why not? I'm not driving.'

48

'Good.' He handed her the money. 'I'll give you a lift home then. What time do you finish?' He could tell that she knew her way round this kind of conversation but could not shake off the impression that she was controlling it and not him.

'Should be three-thirty-ish; it's not too far but I'd be glad of a lift, this weather, thanks.'

She handed him the change, a hint of victory in her eyes.

'Bring your plates back, when you've finished, there's a pet.'

He made slow progress back to Alan; the bar was more crowded now and he had to edge his way through stray business conversations to get there.

'I'll drink this and be off,' Alan said, looking at his watch anxiously.

'I'll hang on a while. Don't mind walking, do you? It's only up the road.'

Alan nodded, disposing of more than half the gin in one gulp.

'Not at all, must go though. Million things to do.' He stood up, polishing off the rest of his drink and shuddering. 'God knows why I like this stuff. See you. Happy hunting.'

Neil was glad to see him go. He changed places so that he could keep an eye on the bar.

So. He wasn't going back to work. Hard to reconcile that with the mad dash to get there that morning – but – to dodge the chain you have to do a lot of ducking and weaving.

His ears brought the noise of the bar into focus, business talk and salesmen's jokes.

They were all standing around in small groups, holding on to their drinks and making their point – or waiting to make their point. No one seemed to be listening.

The talk closed in and then the people closed in as the spaces around the table filled up. He felt a little swimmy. One thought broke away from the chain and came at him separately, strictly against the rules. The afternoon post. He couldn't duck it.

His gaze became snared on all the mouths talking – the speed of their lips out of time with the collective row. Outwardly calm, he sipped at his drink fighting down a small feeling of panic but there was also a feeling of pride that his movements were so relaxed. He turned hunter, found the panic, crushed it.

He got up, winked at the barmaid and left.

1.38 pm

He took a deep breath and watched it escape from him across the clean, cutting air. The snow had turned into a dirty, gritty slush on the road. A watery sun had taken over from the rain in its efforts to clear it. His shadow moved ahead of him to the car, he followed.

He drove aggressively, the alcohol into him now, lifting him up and out of his thoughts; he was skimming above them and you don't have to look down when you're flying.

All systems are GREEN, said a voice. We have ignition, we have LIFT OFF – and the engine roared. He slewed the back wheels round to get through the factory gates, impressing Angela and two other girls who were returning from lunch – late.

Suddenly, *he* was moving through the day. For the first time since leaving work on Friday he was moving through time instead of it being strained through him. We have a GO situation. He glanced at his watch – he had just over an hour and a half – he would leave work at 3.15 to attend to the barmaid.

In a collage of movement and action and decision he skimmed across the time. Everything he did slotted and dovetailed together, nothing required thought or reflection. His decisions were instinctive and his speed pushed him through all the complexities and variations. There was a kind of pent up emotional excitement inside him. The morning was over, this was Monday afternoon – pulling away from the weekend like a boat putting out to sea because the storm is in the harbour and nowhere else. He was flying way, way above it all, in a GO situation and no one could live with the pace or the altitude.... And then, suddenly, there was Sally, with a handful of letters and then she was gone and the letters were on the desk and, on one of the envelopes, there was Jenny's neat handwriting.

And down there, in the playground of thoughts, his thoughts were playing. The rules of the game say that there can only be one chain, this grows and grows: its ungainly size at first a disadvantage but eventually it is large enough to stretch right across the playground so that, ultimately, there is no escape – you can only be the last to be caught – but you are always caught. There can only be more than one chain if you are playing more than one game.

He picked up the envelope and put it in his inside pocket. Glancing at his watch, he reached for his car coat and left. All systems are green.

50

3.35 pm

She was waiting outside the pub, looking cold. The car swooped in for the kerbside, digging its wheels hard into the slush.

'You look cold. Not late am I?' So the talk began, easily and naturally and in this game he was the hunter, pursuing not pursued. She kept looking at him, something in her manner suggesting surprise. Perhaps she could *feel*, sense the difference in him. Perhaps she would be able to fly up there with him, though he doubted it. Jenny had. She had managed to get up there and they were going higher. But then she got shot down, abruptly. She just wasn't there any more. It had brought him down. He lost altitude in his attempts to coax her back up there, talk her out of the sense of failure which seemed to have attached itself to her. All the fight and the dynamism had been sucked out of her and she couldn't get airborne. All so abruptly. Jenny was a career woman and he knew she worked the same way as he did, the pent up emotional excitement carrying her through but he was amazed that she could sustain it for so long, much longer than he could. Shot down, suddenly and when he tried to help – 'Get lost', she said.

'I think we're lost,' she said. 'Sorry, that last road was the one we should have taken. I've only just moved in round here.'

They were driving through bed-sitter land.

'That's OK,' he said. 'Next right and right again will get us there.'

He could feel the letter in his pocket, glad he hadn't opened it; waiting for it had cost him the weekend; now *it* could wait.

'That's the one,' she said looking in her bag for keys. 'By the lamp post.' She snapped the bag shut. He parked the car. He could see the whole afternoon laid out, the evening too probably. He had set himself a deadline to make the game more interesting. He would have her in bed by the six o'clock news; how long they stayed there would depend on how good she was.

They wandered up the path to the front door of the once grand Victorian house and she sorted the right key.

He realized that there had been no question of him not going with her: no 'Thanks for the lift, see you' – nor had there been an actual invitation for him to join her; it was just assumed. Still, he wasn't complaining, he could have handled any coy back tracking on her part very easily.

They entered the semi-dark of the house and there was the smell of dust beneath yesterday's cooking. She led the way upstairs. On the first floor she sorted another key and then they entered.

He was surprised by the bright, airy bed-sitter; it was neat, tidy and nicely decorated.

'Tea or coffee, love?' she asked hanging her coat on the back of the door then moving across the room to light the gas fire.

'Neither thanks, not for me.'

'Well you might as well get your clothes off then.' She disappeared behind a faded screen which made an attempt at sectioning off the kitchen area.

In disbelief, her words shuffled round his mind until an acceptable interpretation emerged. He hung his coat next to hers. Music came from behind the screen and he heard her filling the kettle. The music was slow and sensual.

He sat down, vaguely unsettled. His quarry refused to play the game and she was still in control.

When she came from behind the screen her eyes were laughing. She danced slowly towards him, picking up the feel and subdued rhythm of the music. She had brown eyes; it was the first time he had noticed and the laughter making them sparkle was faintly mocking.

'You're a silly.' She giggled, flipping his tie. 'I meant all the rest too.'

The words shuffled back into their original interpretation, 'Might as well get your clothes off.' He smiled, trying to cover his surprise.

'Oh come on, love.' She laughed aloud now. 'Don't go all coy on me. It's what we're here for, isn't it?'

She sat on his lap and put her arms round his neck. 'Come on,' she said throatily in his ear.

The kettle pulled itself up to boiling point and she left him sitting there, quite unsure how to react.

'Don't look so worried – I'm not going to ask you to pay or anything. I just picked you out, that's all, and we might as well get on with it. I've got to be back at work by eight.'

Neil smiled. And the name of the new game was wresting the initiative.

'I've got a feeling you're going to be good,' she said reappearing with a cup in her hand.

'Fantastic more like.' He got up, took the cup from her and put it on the mantelpiece. 'So why don't you just relax?' His lips made sure she had no time to reply and it was obvious from the way she was kissing that there was no tension in her. Everything about her was relaxed and fluid. He would have preferred a chase but this would have to do and perhaps some of her easy mood would rub off on him.

Neil was still flying, confident that, in taking the initiative from her, he could play an equally interesting game. He broke the kiss, went over to the bed and pulled back the covers; she joined him at the bedside and continued with the kiss. The music on the radio had degenerated into a trough of talking. He broke the kiss again.

'Why don't you go and kill that?' he said nodding at the voice. She did. '. . . and in ten minutes we'll be taking you over to the news room for the four o'clock news and then stay tuned for . . .' Dead. Night falling, the sound of a car passing by. She returned with her coffee: again he took it from her, putting it on the bedside table next to the clock. He kissed her.

Her hand reached up to the back of his neck, her fingers cool and gentle. Electricity shot wavy lines down his spine; he responded via the kiss and his now hard penis pressing against her.

Whilst still maintaining the kiss, she moved away enough for her fingers to glide down over his chest, across his stomach, pausing at his zip then taking it on down. Her hand slipped inside, moving up and down with incredible gentleness and so slowly. It was as if the music she had danced to was still playing. The feeling was beautiful but it wasn't scoring him many points in the game so his hands began to stray. He let the nails on the fingers of both his hands trace the length of her spine until they came to rest on her bottom. It was just as nice as he had hoped. He spread his hands on her buttocks and pulled her close. That trapped her hand, she retrieved it. He jerked her blouse out of the waistband of her skirt and unbuttoned it. He took it from her.

He was sure she knew all about the game they were playing and he claimed victory, as slowly, in keeping with what had gone before, he stripped her clothes from her. When he had finished taking them from her she stood there shivering slightly. She looked beautiful naked. From then on she became more passive.

Neil undressed and joined her in bed. She seemed less relaxed but he was flying and began to give full rein to all his expertise. Using every trick and wile, touch and caress, he brought her to the point where she was ready to accept him, and soon after brought it all to a very satisfactory conclusion.

53

He rolled off her and lay by her side. Night had almost finished its long winter fall into afternoon. A streetlight came on suddenly, splashing the outline of the window across the chimney breast. He let out a deep sigh. She had drawn from him the very best and victory is always sweet.

'Good?' he said at last, smiling.

'Technically – that was brilliant.'

He grinned and then the word technically bothered him. He resumed his study of the ceiling, unsmiling.

'Technically?'

'You were brilliant – considering how few chapters of the manual you actually read.' The acid disappointment in her voice was unmistakable; it retreated as she said, 'Set the alarm for about seven pet, would you? I'm going to have a nap.'

She turned away from him and pulled the clothes around her. He set the alarm without thinking, then lay staring out the dark trying to make sense of her disappointment. Another chain building? To dodge and weave from across the playground? And how much running to avoid this one, how much to duck the other one? And, like the alarm, they were primed and set and running.

He was coming in to land. He dare not question her disappointment, afraid of what he might hear and unwilling to be criticized on his performance in bed, where he was strongest – and most vulnerable.

Her breathing was steady and his eyes were tired. Lulled by the quiet hiss of the gas fire and the sleep sounds in the room he ducked into sleep, encouraged by the fact that later – alone – he knew he would sleep only fitfully. The figures on the digital alarm changed to 4.25 as sleep reached up and pulled him down.

6.49 pm

He awoke with panic staring right back at him out of the blind darkness. He sat up violently and the streetlight shadows, the glow from the fire, cut back into focus. The thought chains were running out there beneath the night – and he wasn't. They were coming.

He was out of bed and dressing hurriedly, conscious of the sweat on his brow and the coldness of the room despite the false glow of the fire. Everything was so urgent. He scrabbled in frantic silence for a sock on the floor as, up there above him on the bedside table, the green, liquid figures of the alarm swam: two green dots stabbing seconds out across the room.

She was breathing heavily and, as his eyes grew used to the light further, he could see her vague outline, curled beneath the covers like a question mark.

He finished dressing, driven by the need to get away. He paused by the clock; it was due to go off in another ten minutes. He clicked the slide across to save it the trouble. Let her sleep.

The car twisted and turned through the side streets. Streetlights and slushed up snow, houses with drawn curtains, standing shoulder to shoulder. He pushed the car on, eventually picking up the main road, glad of the orange lights and the movement there.

A stream of cars was trooping into the city and he joined the queue without impatience, now ahead and clear of the panic.

Just one of those boring, liberated women, that was all. Afraid to admit her enjoyment in case she was classed as a ... What was the phrase her sort were always using? ... a sex object. Much too easy, anyway. The words were tall beneath the lights but they cast down shadows beneath each one.

Jenny was liberated. They had made love only once, there hadn't been the opportunity since, had there? She had gone to the North, lecturing at a conference or something and when she returned it was already too late. Shot down. He went to see her; she was using a flat, had left her husband and she was free. He had met him. Her husband had been in the pub one lunchtime when he took her out to lunch, by chance it seemed, though he was never sure if she had planned it that way. How she had looked then, before she went away, her hair shining and black, piled on top of her head, large deep brown eyes – stunningly beautiful. So proud to have her next to him. But when she returned from the North ... His forehead creased up as he remembered and then realized the chain had caught him up, was encircling him and the car had slowed to thirty miles per hour.

He stamped on the accelerator and shot forwards, streaking ahead of a rusty, old Mini on the inside which had just overtaken him. He got clear and moved out into the fast lane, shaking off the Mini and his thoughts.

He laughed suddenly, thinking of the barmaid still asleep. Hope she's late for work – serve her bloody well right.

He headed off the main road for the factory. It was as good an excuse not to go home as any – there he would not be alone and it was harder to stay out in front, alone.

There was still the letter – unopened – but now it *had* to wait; he could not risk another 'Get lost'.

Stan waved him on past the lodge and he screamed the wheels round into the staff car-park – deserted except for Alan's car. As he walked towards the factory, he could hear its roar, see the slabs of light it was putting out. He glanced at his watch as he let it all envelop him.

7.01 pm

Sally looked absently out of the window, not that there was much to see, just the light pushing outwards from the factory and then the dark lying on top of what was left of the snow.

There was nothing more she could do tonight, really. She was tired but reluctant to go home. Bette was down the corridor finishing off some photocopying for Alan. She had made her promise that she would be gone when she got back but not to tell Angela. Angela didn't have an early start in the morning.

She could hear the sports car long before she could see it but then its lights darted around the corner, slicing across the dark and making the snow momentarily yellow.

She watched him hurry across the car-park. He must have forgotten something. All of the girls raved about him but she wasn't at all sure that she liked him. He was funny and sometimes made her laugh and at first she had loved his flattery but there was a kind of immaculate arrogance about him. She could only imagine him wanting things, never giving them. . . . He treated her like a child, anyway, unlike Alan.

There was still guilt attached to her thoughts of him, but it was easier to push away now.

7.02 pm

The noise, the warmth and the clattering urgency of it all pulled him into the building. As if taken there by convection, his spirits rose up again as the sheer pace of the shop floor got inside him. As he walked along the passageway the colourful images caught his eye, bright and merry as they moved from one stage of production to the next.

He saw Bob as he moved towards the stairs. He held his fist aloft in a gladiatorial salute and mouthed the word 'Go!' across at him. Bob grinned, probably thinking that enthusiasm had been the cause of the gesture.

He climbed the stairs, making straight for Alan's office. He entered without knocking. Alan was slumped over the desk, his head resting on his arm, his other hand made a claw on a sheet of figures.

Neil sucked in his breath sharply. Heart attack!

'*Alan!*'

He stirred, his hand turning from a claw to a fist.

'Oh Christ,' he moaned, his voice thick with sleep and anguish. 'Did I sleep?' Alan sat up, stiff, still seeing sleep.

'Oh shit,' he said thickly. 'I slept.' There was an almost childlike disappointment in his voice. His right eye was badly bloodshot. He stared fixedly at the papers on his desk, seemingly only vaguely aware of Neil's presence.

Neil smiled. Relieved, he left the room quietly, heading for the coffee machine. He returned with two cups and plonked one in front of Alan. He seemed at least three parts conscious now, smiling.

'Was it you who was in here – just?'

Neil nodded.

'Must have dozed off.'

'Mm. Given the evidence, that seems likely.'

'What brings you here, anyway? It must be . . .' He glanced at his watch. 'Strewth! It must be nearly five past seven. God what a day. I feel funny.'

'You look it too. You've got a big red blotch on the side of your face where you slept and the last time I saw an eye like that I was nineteen and getting over a three day drunk.'

Alan laughed quietly. 'Bloodshot is it? Oh well, that must mean it's Christmas then.' He drank the coffee thirstily. 'Anyway, now you're here – are you going to help? This is the question. There's so much work to do, mate, it's *silly*.'

'D'you mean you're not going to drag yourself off somewhere and die for twelve hours or so in bed? What time are you working till?'

'Ten o'clock, -ish. The factory runs till then. Had a really good afternoon. We're going round the clock tomorrow. The union lapped it up. Two shifts all the week, then Saturday and Sunday we all pile into Despatch, pack it and shift it out of there. They even agreed to work on till ten tonight.'

'Bless their little hearts,' said Neil cynically. 'And I don't suppose the money had anything to do with it.'

Alan threw the empty cup at the waste bin – missed.

'Ah, come on Neil, we've got a good team down there, thanks to Jim. You're just a cynic.'

'That's right.' He smiled. 'Anyway, now I'm here, better help I suppose. Backs to the wall, all that crap. What needs doing?'

'More coffee for starters – then maybe you could help me analyse some orders. I'm doing a random sample to check the projection. I'm due for a spell on the fork lift at eight. The driver couldn't stay tonight on such short notice, but he's OK the rest of the week.'

'*You!* On the fork lift truck?' Neil stared at him, incredulous, then burst out laughing. 'Can you drive one?'

Alan joined in the laughter. 'It's not *that* funny, man. Sure I can drive one. Jim taught me one Saturday. Great fun it was. I practically redesigned the entire factory in an hour. I got the hang of it eventually. Anyway, it'll give the lads something to smile about.'

Neil shook his head, feigning seriousness.

'Well – you've finally flipped then, Henson. It's a sad case. I suppose I'd better stay now just to see how the "lads" react when they realize their hero has gone bananas.'

'Two coffees and fingers to you. Come on, Telford, you're working in a *real* department now, not the Mickey Mouse outfit you're used to.'

Neil laughed again, getting up. Alan was flying too.

'Talking of Mickey Mouse – where's Broughton – haven't got him emptying the bins, have you?'

58

'No, he applied but I didn't reckon he was up to it, so I sent him home – can't stand the pace. By the way, how did you get on with the barmaid?'

Neil made a crude gesture and grinned.

'Magic. Best I've had all week!' He fished in his pockets for change and moved towards the door, in this mood it was difficult to find a gap in Alan's thoughts to make an exit through. He had become suddenly serious.

'Y'know Neil, I was thinking. All this eleventh hour crisis stuff is all very well, but it hit me, right in the middle of it – *why*? Why is demand so high?'

Neil stood in the doorway. Standing face on to the door-frame he tapped on the woodwork and tried to appear as if he was thinking of reasons. He already knew the answer.

'Sometimes these things happen,' he offered.

'Not if the catalogues are withdrawn from the shops, they don't, they can't. I made a few phone calls. Only four of our salesmen have actually withdrawn the books – that means we're still selling in the other five territories.'

Neil signified surprise. It was genuine too. Alan had got there all by himself, just as he'd hoped.

'All this is Broughton's patch, isn't it?' he asked innocently.

'Too true it is. The four who did stop the books are old hands; they'd do it without instruction – the new boys wouldn't. I reckon our Edgar forgot to put the memo out, telling them to. I hope so, 'cos I'm going to nail the old fox to the factory gates if that's right.'

'Mm – looks like you've got him. Are we still selling?'

'No. I took steps to deal with that. No wonder sales are so high, we're the only people in the market place daft enough to be still taking orders this close on Christmas.'

Neil nodded in agreement.

'Take care,' he warned. 'Line him up right before you nail him.'

He closed the door and as he walked down the corridor he whispered the word 'Perfect'.

He had wondered whether or not it would be necessary to prime Alan but he had got there on his own initiative and it would be him firing the bullets not Neil; he was clear. Edgar was out of the game.

He slotted the money into the machine, tapping on its sides. Now the only way he could be dragged into it was through Sally.

There was the sound of high heels coming up the stairs.

7.11 pm

He appraised Angela frankly as she walked towards him. She had looked very dispirited at first but was smiling now she had seen him. If you didn't know her, she'd be perfect. She always wore just the right clothes. She had excellent taste. And she was one of those rare girls who could wear her hair in a different style each day and each one would be right. She had rich shoulder length hair – sandy brown. A pretty face, perhaps overdoing the make-up, and a lovely, head-turning figure. There was only one thing wrong with her ...

'Hello. Are you working late too? This overtime is all very well – I didn't really want to do it but Bette sort of came the heavy, you know what she's like – but I think it's a bit much – I feel quite ill, actually – I mean they ought to make some arrangements for food – I haven't eaten a thing since lunchtime....'

... and that was her voice. Not only was it sweet and over-girlish but it poured out of her in a seemingly endless string.

'So how about a steak then?' he said impulsively, right over the top of what she was saying. That stopped her.

'A steak?'

'There are two big ones sitting at home in the fridge.'

'Well ...' She smiled, making an attempt at shyness by averting her eyes. He knew she had been waiting for the chance for weeks.

'All right then,' she said in a giggly, mischievous voice.

'Fine. We'll pop into the Roebuck for a drink on the way.'

He picked up the coffees.

'You go and tell the Snow Queen then, stand up for yourself. I'll dump these and see you back here in a couple of minutes.'

Another giggle was her reply. He wandered off jauntily to Alan's office. He went in quickly putting both cups on the desk.

'Sorry, Alan – got a date – forgot everything about it. Must go. Don't work too hard. See you tomorrow.'

He left hurriedly, closing the door. He held it shut for a count of five, then opened it again, popping his head inside.

60

'No, Alan, that's not an accurate description actually and to prove it I'll bring my birth certificate in. Both parents are named.'

He caught a reasonably good-natured 'Sod off' as he closed the door again. Alan would cope.

He walked along the corridor facing the prospect of an evening with Angela but it would be interesting to see if the barmaid had turned up for work yet and having Angela at his side would be no disgrace at all.

He collected the briefcase from his office, locked the door carefully and whistled as he sauntered along.

7.15 pm

Footsteps on the stairs and the sound of Angela's chatter made Sally turn her head as she left Bette's office. They were leaving. She looked out over the shop floor on her way to Alan's office. It was strange being there so late. The night pressed against the enormous sky-light windows, peering in and the factory looked different, somehow, lit only by the countless fluorescent lights hanging down.

She knocked and entered.

'Ah – well timed. There's a cup of coffee here you can drink, help yourself. I sort of got left with it, amongst other things. Have a seat. Are those the first schedules?'

'Yes, I meant to bring them earlier.' She had brought them earlier but heard Neil's voice. She preferred to be alone with him. Her heart beat a little faster now he was actually looking at her. He smiled.

'Has Angela done those memos yet?'

'Er – no, she's just gone home but Bette is finishing them now, I think.'

The slight scene between Bette and Angela had served to make Bette forget she had told her to go home. Sally had been determined to see him just once more before going.

'I see,' he said thoughtfully, studying the schedules.

'I'm free at the moment, is there anything I can do here?'

His face lit up and she was glad she had offered.

'You could analyse those orders if you like,' he said eagerly, but then he hesitated. 'But it's late – oughtn't you be going home? Won't your parents worry?'

She felt a brief resentment at being treated like a child.

'No, that's OK. I phoned them earlier, said I'd be late.' She felt anything but a child when he looked at her. She noticed his blood-shot eye as he glanced away and then how tired he looked.

She picked up a bundle of orders and cleared a space on the corner of his desk. He came round, leaning over her as he explained what he wanted her to do.

They worked in silence for a long time. Finally she came to the last order with a sigh of relief. He looked up, smiling.

'All done?'

She nodded. It had been difficult to concentrate with him so near.

'I've just got to do the totals,' she said, returning the smile.

'No, that's all right love, I'll do those later. I'd be much happier if you went home, you know.'

'Do you think we'll do it? I mean, get all this work through on time?' she asked, avoiding the issue.

'Anybody's guess at the moment, love. Probably. We've made a good start, anyway.'

'Everyone seems so *involved* downstairs – no one seems to be moaning like they usually do.'

'Yes, they've been great. The response is the best part of this bloody awful day.'

'Alan? I heard something today and I was wondering if it's true.'

'Another rumour?'

'It was about Bette. I heard she might be leaving.'

He looked surprised.

'Really? Where did you hear that?'

'It was just something someone heard her say on the phone – about arranging for her replacement.'

'Shouldn't think it's true. Doesn't seem likely. No, I can't see it myself. She knows this place inside out. Write that one off as a rumour if I were you.'

She smiled, gazing at him. He glanced at his watch.

'I should have been on the shop floor five minutes ago, on the fork lift. The factory will stop – can't have that.' He stood up. 'Now, young lady – will you *please* go home?'

'Oh but ...'

'You'll be starting early tomorrow won't you? And it's going to be a long, long week. You've been a great help, I appreciate it but I'll need your help all the rest of the week too ... OK?'

'I suppose I ought to ... really.' She got up and dropped the empty cup into the bin. She walked to the door.

'Oh Sally – thanks and – well done.'

She left in some confusion unable to stop herself blushing. She knew she was in love with him and the idea frightened her but the thoughts about him being older and married paled into the shadows – thrown there by the fierceness of this feeling inside her.

9.30 pm

Grounded. As Neil carried the meals through to the lounge, Angela brushed past him, on her way to the bathroom. He could hear her being sick. He put the plates on the dining-table, blew out the candles and sat on the sofa. Grounded. He picked up the evening paper but his eyes skimmed right over the page without catching on anything. He slammed it down on the sofa angrily. He had put too much drink into her, his judgement must be failing him. The barmaid hadn't shown up at the Roebuck and he had tried to fend off the broader and broader hints Angela was putting out about how hungry she was. Eventually they had come away.

Angela had been very quiet as they drove to his flat which was a kind of relief but it wasn't what she was there for. What was she there for?

He got up, turned on the TV – a commentator's high-pitched voice immediately jarred into him so he turned the sound down and let the picture run. He sat down again, restless. She was there to chatter away any possibility of it all closing in on him. Dodge and weave – keep ahead of it. Grounded now in his own flat. She wasn't there to spite the barmaid nor to repair an ego which had not been damaged.

He looked round, she was standing in the doorway, unsteadily, her eyes streaming, her mascara running. She looked, fleetingly, like a clown. He felt a sudden tenderness towards her. He got up and went to her, putting his arms round her. She sagged against him.

'Come on,' he said quietly and led her to the bedroom. He picked her up and laid her gently on the bed. She was almost asleep. He returned to the lounge.

It was his own fault, he should have stayed at work; he was flying there. The grease was beginning to form on the plates as he walked past the table.

He watched them moving across the TV screen. Highlights of an indoor show jumping event. Jumping against the clock. Seconds and tenths of seconds moving on the screen. Minutes passed. He waited for the next horseman, for the clock to come back and start all over again.

He turned his head, glanced at the meals on the table, looked back at the TV – the clock was running. Jenny had hardly touched the meal he had cooked; she was so tired, so unbelievably tense. Dressed in a loose sweater and faded jeans, her hair straggly, she told him what a mess she had made of the lectures and of things beginning to go wrong with her career. Explicitly, frankly, she told him as if she *wanted* to drive him away. It was a very strained evening. When she wasn't talking of her failures she was talking of her husband and Neil didn't want to know.

The horse virtually demolished the final fence, recovered unsteadily, then raced for the line. The clock stopped. He watched. It wasn't the Jenny he knew nor the one he wanted. But he had tried. Tried to lift her out of and above the sticky sense of failure which was so suddenly clinging to her. He had tried to make love to her thinking this would lift her but she had pushed him away, disgusted. Get lost.

He got up suddenly, went to the bedroom. Angela lay there, her skirt ridden up over her thighs – he paused, froze. She had beautiful legs. He gazed at her. She was wearing black panties. No chatter now, her face calm, her breathing heavy.

He shook his head, went quickly to the wardrobe and took his suit jacket off the hanger. He put it on. Her legs caught his eye again in the wardrobe door as it swung closed. He went to the ottoman and fetched a blanket. He stood at the bedside, gently pulling down her skirt, avoiding touching her; then he covered her over and left the bedroom quickly.

The meals, the silent television, the crumpled evening paper – he turned out the light and closed the door on them all.

10.24 pm

Sixty miles per hour on the dual carriageway heading North for the motorway. He turned on the radio, turned it up loud and watched the orange lights pass by. Motorway one mile, said the sign. 'Stay tuned for more golden oldies,' said the disc jockey over the fading music. He pressed the accelerator gently. The roads were empty, jewelled with frost but the clouds above threatened to wash it away. Seventy-five. The commercials on the radio stopped, the music started – electric guitars and a voice singing '*Hey Joe, I heard you shot your woman down, shot her down to the ground.*' And the thought chain started back up again, darting out from behind the words.

He reached for the switch on the radio but thought better of it as the motorway island loomed up. He stepped off the accelerator, squeezed the brake, changed gear, slowed.

He didn't shoot her down, maybe her husband did, maybe she turned kamikazi, but he didn't. Second gear. Stop. Waiting for a heavy lorry to snake its tired way round the island. And when she started to fall she just kept on falling, down and down and she wouldn't respond. Fingers of panic as he watched on, feeling helpless, inadequate and remote.

'*Hey Joe? Where you gonna run to now, where you gonna go?*'

He flipped the switch. First. Second gear. The motorway sign, To the North. Third off the island and down the approach road, hard on the accelerator. The motorway was empty. Fourth gear, moving out into the centre lane. Getting clear and beginning to leave Jenny behind. But he had tried. Eighty-five miles per hour and counting. Ninety-eight. Overdrive. All systems are GREEN.

His thoughts turned to Alan. He had really surprised him, responding to the crisis well, hitting the gas pedal hard. He had really expected him to fold up – what to Alan had been an unexpected rush of orders should have been enough to push him over. The unforeseen – Jim's death – should have sealed it, sending morale on the shop floor to an all time low and leaving the factory struggling to attain normal output levels. With Alan taken out of the game and Edgar due to be taken out at any time, it would have left him home and clear. That's how it had looked this morning.

Alan would be out of fuel by the end of the week but it couldn't be relied on. On Friday the spotlight would be on Alan – and Myers, of course, but he didn't know what time it was. It might be necessary to attack Alan, he thought. Having mobilized him against Edgar he might now have to take some of the shine from him. He was going to be an asset though when he was Managing Director. He had proved how hard he could work and as long as he continued to prove it there'd be no problem.

There was no problem with Bette either, apparently. When Angela had still been chattering – before her mouth seized up – she told him that Bette was moving on. That would save him the effort though he felt a tinge of disappointment – he would have liked to have brought her down a few notches.

He pushed the car on a little faster. It would all be OK once he was appointed. How many times was it in recent weeks he had felt the need to gun the car down the motorway? When he had first got the car he would often race it the thirty miles or so to the motorway café, keeping a mental note of the time it took. But, recently, he'd been doing it to escape the tossing sleeplessness and the pitchfork thoughts which turned him over in the dark.

A well lit sign stepped up out of the night and told him that the café was now only a mile away. He eased off on the accelerator and, as the car began to lose speed, he became aware of the envelope in the inside pocket of his jacket.

10.48 pm

The café wasn't as busy as he'd hoped, in fact it wasn't busy at all.

'Coffee, please, strong and black.'

The old man behind the counter put down the book he had been engrossed in, frowning. Neil looked around the almost deserted café. A group of drivers were playing cards, another was sitting alone gazing out into the night. A young couple laughed quietly in the corner. The place was dead – and quiet.

The old man shoved the drink across the counter, took his money and then returned wearily to the pages of his book.

Neil sat down, weary himself, suddenly. There was an evening paper on the seat by his side. He put it on the table – tried to read it, failed. He took the envelope from his pocket, propped it up against the cruet and looked at the neat writing. It would be easy to leave it there, drive back without it. It would be sensible. It probably contained another 'Get lost'. He couldn't face that so why not walk away from it? Jenny was probably angry because he had been to see her husband about her, told him about the state she was in. He didn't want to know and said it was *his* responsibility. It had meant screwing up his pride, going there. He hadn't been trying to dump her, at least, not before he spoke to him he hadn't. It was their mess, not his and it looked as if it would be a long time before she was flying again.

He had lost so much altitude. It was a pity you couldn't dump thoughts as easily as you could people. He couldn't stop himself from wondering what was happening to her.

He looked across at the young couple. They were so obviously in love, talking softly, sometimes laughing, sometimes just looking at each other. They were totally unaware of him or anyone else in the room. As Neil watched he realized that it had never been like that for him – not with Jenny or anyone. He had always tried to make it look like that on the outside, but, inside, it had never been like that.

He shrugged off the envy. It probably wasn't like it for the lad inside either. He was probably just geeing her along and hoping to score. And even if he wasn't they were just kids – still immature enough to believe in all that rubbish.

He looked away, still envious. He concentrated on the table, pushing stray sugar grains around, making patterns.

A gush of cold air beat a temporary path through the air conditioning. He froze as she came in. She hadn't noticed him yet. She didn't look like a barmaid now. He watched as she walked to the counter, carrying a suitcase. She had her hair pinned up and she was wearing tight jeans tucked into boots, a white polo-neck jumper and a denim jacket.

She smiled as she came towards him. He looked at her, completely off guard, unsure what stance or attitude to take. She dumped the suitcase carelessly by the side of the table. Putting her coffee down she sat opposite him.

'Y'know I had a gut feeling I'd be seeing you again. Never imagined it would be this soon, of course. What *is* your name, by the way?'

'Neil. What are you doing here?'

'Looking for another lift. My last one was getting off next junction.'

'What about your job?' he asked, uneasily.

'I lost it. I was late.' Her eyes said 'thanks a lot', but she continued to smile and he continued to feel at a disadvantage.

'Bit unfair,' he said. 'Surely they can't...'

'Oh, I was due for the bullet, anyway. The landlord's wife didn't take to me, maybe because he did. She thought I'd got my hand in the till too – but she'll have to think again there. I heard them arguing – "Must have reliable staff over Christmas",' she mimicked. 'I couldn't make out what he said, he was really wet. So, the bullet, and here I am.'

'I came to see you, earlier,' he said.

'Why?'

He left the question unanswered. He got up abruptly and just left her there. He got a glass of milk and returned.

'Where are you heading?'

'North – just North. I travel a lot. Jobs here and there. Rooms, digs, hotels if I have to. Work and save and move on.'

'A drifter? You?' He couldn't keep surprise or the hint of contempt from his voice.

'I've travelled up and down, North to South, South to North – oh – three times now I suppose, different routes, always different towns.

'Bit dangerous isn't it?'

'Predatory males, you mean?' She smiled. 'No, not in the least. I've got a black belt in karate, orange in judo.'

He had run out of things to say. Her effect on him was strange, neutralizing him. He was never able to wrest control from her. He had claimed victory in the afternoon but it had been a hollow one.

He felt trapped, as he had in the pub. The letter from Jenny in front of him, the barmaid behind that. All the ducking and weaving had brought him right up against them just the same. *'Hey Joe, where you gonna run to now?'*

'What's your name?'

'Guess,' she said back at him immediately.

'How can I guess, I mean...?' He was exasperated.

'What do I look like? Mary? Susan? Martha?'

'Judi,' he said not wishing to play the game but playing it.

'That's it! That's my name – Judi.'

He knew it wasn't but – what the hell, what did it matter? He dimly realized this was probably the point she was making.

The questions he wanted answering were lining themselves up, daring him to ask them, collect in the answers. Get up and walk away from her, leave the answers behind and that look in her eyes, the quiet calmness of her manner, the confidence.

'Sorry you lost your job,' he said, meaning it.

'I'm not. It's Christmas – plenty of temporary work about.'

'Why move on, then?'

'I looked in the evening paper, nothing appealed, so I'm moving.'

'What was wrong – with this afternoon?'

It was as if the questions had got tired of waiting, as if he hadn't asked.

'Wrong? Nothing. You were brilliant – didn't I say? Why – did *you* think there was anything wrong?'

Damn her!

'No – great, I thought – but I sensed you weren't exactly happy.'

'Ah.' She nodded slowly, sipped at her coffee and said nothing further but her eyes were mocking him. A tide of impatience swept through him.

'I don't *understand* you! What's your game?'

'And I don't see why you're so uptight about it. It was great, wasn't it? You just said so. Didn't I make the right noises or something?'

She wasn't going to be led and it came to him sharply that *she* might get up and walk away, take the answers with her. He broke cover.

'OK, it was my game. I saw you and decided to have you by the six o'clock news, OK? Is that what you want to hear? It was my game – you didn't play – I didn't enjoy it – you won.'

'It was afterwards you didn't enjoy it, surely?'

He dropped his head in admission.

'It's afterwards that you *really* enjoy it, isn't it? Oh Neil that was wonderful! Thank you!'

He couldn't stop himself from smiling at the way she had changed her voice.

'Yeah, right. Anything you say, Judi. Sorry I disappointed you Judi but – why did you pick me out, Judi?'

She smiled, affectionately, with humour and warmth. It was infectious but he kept the smile from his lips.

'Come on, Neil,' she coaxed. 'Don't take it all so seriously. Sex is funny, isn't it? Isn't it fun? I picked you out because I thought you might be fun.'

'You were fun, why wasn't I?'

'Because of the game, I suppose. Games have rules that must be obeyed. They have winners and – losers, of course.'

She hadn't lost the game, he thought, simply withdrawn from it. No contest.

'In my experience,' she said. 'There are just two types of men and I separate them by the way they view women. You imagine a group of young boys, just at puberty, looking at a pretty girl from a street corner. Some never leave that group, no matter what.'

He was puzzled.

'So?'

'All their actions and crude references and responses are played for the boys.'

'I'm still not with you. What's more natural than that?'

'Nothing – at that age. Each of them is measuring himself up against the rest, seeking their approval. This is where the rules are written. A few will grow up, most won't.'

'And the ones who grow up?'

'Don't play games.'

He smiled, ruefully. She returned the smile. The young couple got up and left, still talking and completely oblivious to the world around them. He watched them go and when his eyes returned to Judi she was standing and on her way to the counter. She returned with another coffee.

'So?'

'So, there we are then.' She still wasn't going to be led.

'So you think I was pleasing the boys this afternoon?'

'You know what I mean. Think about it.'

It was probably the strangest conversation he had ever had, certainly with a woman.

'Still, at least I was brilliant, even if only technically.'

'Yes you were and that's what made me so sad. But there's more to it than technique. Once you thought I was ready it was wham, bam and not even a thank-you ma'am. It was all for you. Sad. A bit like being served the most incredibly subtle hors d'oeuvres and then

70

having the main course whisked away from you. You still wanted the dessert, of course.'

'I suppose I can't complain then – two courses out of three.'

'You can't – no. It was wanting the third which exposed you. At least you wanted my approval, for whatever reason. Some couldn't care less about the dessert anyway which, in some ways, is even worse.'

He tried to make sense out of what she had been saying but it was difficult to imagine it without the rules. Satisfaction was guaranteed either way so where was the incentive? The rules made it interesting. What was wrong with being a natural winner?

He looked over at the men still playing cards and the one on his own still absorbed by whatever it was he could see beyond the window pane. It was raining heavily now outside.

'Why don't you stay?' he said on impulse. 'I could probably find you a job at the factory.'

'Yes, it does seem a shame, now we've made a start, doesn't it? But, no, I'm moving on. I'll find out where that driver is going. I did a "moonlight" from my digs and – yes, I'm sure you've got a spare room but, no thanks.'

He grinned and then thought of Angela beneath the blanket.

'And anyway, she might not approve.'

He was startled.

'She?'

'The one you're hung up on.'

He closed up. He had been beginning to feel less threatened by her.

'You saw that too!' It wasn't a question.

'Maybe that's why I picked you out.'

The driver got up suddenly and made to leave. She saw him go and stood up.

'That's another story,' he said. 'Take care.'

She kissed him tenderly, then ruffled his hair.

'Think about it – give it a try. What have you got to lose? Must go – I'll miss my lift ... goodbye.'

He listened to the sound of her heels, disappearing. She might not get a lift, might come back. He looked at the folded paper and the minutes passed. She did not return. At the bottom of the page the word 'suicide' came into focus and Jenny's name. He watched as his hand reached out and dragged the paper nearer. It was hardly necessary to read the three line story. He did. His eyes closed. He held his breath. It finally escaped in one long, inevitable sigh.

His eyes opened and he stood up. He walked away slowly and left the letter where it was.

Monday Night

11.55 pm

Sally crossed the chilly landing clutching her dressing-gown to her. She entered the warmth of her room, relaxed after a bath and utterly tired.

In bed she curled up into a tight ball and let the swimmy, sleepy feeling wash over her luxuriously. Calm thoughts lowered her down towards sleep as she saw Alan, tired and harassed with everyone and everything against him, except her. Together they pushed it all away and won through. He was so proud of her, so in love with her. But the Town Hall clock was striking in the distance, coming nearer, until she was there, standing beneath it – alone as it chimed madly although it hadn't found the hour.

When the big hand reached the top it stretched down from the clock tower and pointed at her, chanting 'It's time, time for *you*!' over and over. Then there was the grinning radiator grill between the blinding headlights, the relief of seeing someone she knew and talking, but then the hand came at her again, was pawing at her, trying to reach up her skirt. Breaking free and running and running and running. Alan caught her, held her and it was all right. He slowed everything and he listened, only, he looked a bit like Jim but it really was Alan and he held her firmly and made her empty it all out because it was too horrible to keep inside.

Sally slept on.

A click – the light went out – chased out by the immediate heaviness of the dark. Edgar waited for his thoughts to follow or at least to calm. He heard his sister coming to bed. He lay there gazing at the space where he thought the ceiling ought to be, picturing her in her dressing-gown, a cup of cocoa in her hand. He had left her in front of the TV screen, watching the empty people there.

The thoughts returned as the dark began to weaken, letting the streetlight creep into the room and shadows fall around its familiar shapes. Where was Rita now? His wife – former wife all those years ago, and his son, where was he, where was Lawrence?

Stop! Edgar almost cried it aloud. It was so loud in his mind he lay there and wondered whether or not he had actually spoken. The word stood up there against the semi-dark but couldn't show the anguish or the anger, just up there in the shadows.

He twisted round on his side, trying to catch at sleep but it moved just out of reach. Where were all the people who had left him?

He turned over again. Where was sleep?

Neil pushed the key in the lock, twisted it. The lounge flickered in silver-blue light. He walked over to the silent television and switched it off. In the sudden dark, the tube was grey and fading. He walked carefully past the evening paper on the settee and the meals on the table. It had been there all the time, in the paper, and he had run thirty miles to read it.

He went to the bedroom, undressing carelessly in the dark. He could see Angela's form beneath the blanket, still fully clothed. Her breathing reached out from the shadows. Naked he crawled under the blanket. She turned in her sleep facing him – and as her arm moved he ducked beneath it so that it came around him.

Behind tightly closed eyes he saw Judi, the lower part of her face veiled by shadow. She was talking and he knew she was saying all the things he had heard her say but he could only see her eyes. He would never see her again – she looked so like Jenny with her hair pinned up. A few hours ago he had *wanted* never to see her again. Life is so perverse, with the wishes it grants and those it does not.

He saw them all together, at the meeting table, all looking at him, puzzled. 'Is *this* Neil Telford?' they said, their voices sad and dismayed. Bette sitting at the head of the table showed no surprise, as if she had known from the start. Sally was standing in a corner, quietly undressing. Over it all there was a rhythmic drumming, persistent, unceasing. He kept repeating the gesture he had made when Alan asked about the barmaid, repeating it over and over as he looked at Sally. And outside, down on a street corner Judi was deep in conversation with Jenny and the drumming grew louder and louder and then there was just Jenny and Jenny and Jenny....

He woke suddenly, the noise persisted. Rain on the window. A nightmare galloping away, the rain had come again.

74

He lay in the dark and listened until it eased but the pictures of Jenny would not.

He moved closer to Angela, crying quietly.

'The rain's easing, but the snow has all gone now,' she said, disappointed.

'Good.' Alan watched as she brushed her hair. He was sitting up in bed, naked, his head back against the quilted bed head. The room was soft and warm beneath the muted lights.

'I wanted a white Christmas,' she said. He admired her hair and the way it swirled when she shook her head.

'There'll be plenty more, I expect.'

He never tired of watching her. Some people, they needed a quota of the sea or green fields and flowers but he just needed her. There had been a single moment during the afternoon when he had looked at Sally and realized that he could fall in love with her. It had shocked him but, as Nancy turned from the dressing-table mirror to face him he realized that she looked like a slightly older version of Sally.

'Love you,' he said. She smiled and came to sit on the edge of the bed. She eased the straps of her nightdress from her shoulders, sexily. Her eyes questioned him.

'Sorry, love,' he said sadly. 'Too wound up, I wouldn't make it.' She looked disappointed.

'But ...' he said smiling again, 'no reason why you shouldn't.'

She slipped into bed and his arms, and the clock on the bedside table looked on. Outside, in the midnight quiet there was the sound of footsteps, running. The rain had stopped. She relaxed down into the bed and his hand ran over her body.

Breathless in the night. Everything halts after the torrent – watchful in case it ventures back, and the stone streets stand, impassive, secretly itching to shake off the rain.

David walked down the street and the stillness wrapped itself round his surging heartbeat, trying to quieten it. Breaking the quiet was the slow pitter-pat as the rain dripped off the trees into broken pools all down the tree-lined street – waiting for the mirror calm to resurface.

David walked through a puddle without noticing. The thumping heartbeat in his ears was receding gradually and the noise he had

75

made, slamming the front door, was now seven, eight, nine houses back.

Back there – his house, with every light burning. Their house, at the turn of the day, beneath midnight. Beneath his feet, the pavement glistening and his step quickening. From the house, chasing him, came the thought of what he had done. The rhythm of his footsteps quickened, quickened.

He looked round but you can't see a thought, except on someone else's face and there was just an empty street with a brightly lit house at the end of it.

He ran, from house to house, streetlight to streetlight, he ran ahead of his breath, faster. Round the corner another street, faster, chased by his own footsteps, echoing in the hush and running from the thought of what he had done.

If I can't make you listen, I can make you watch but for both our sakes you must not only see but understand.

The colour is sepia. Twilight. Ahead — the immense plain lies, empty, beneath a falling sky. A low moon, stars, silence. From this lone hill top you can see back over the leafless forest and hear the sound coming from it, ripping and tearing at the complex tangle, crashing to free itself from the interstranded web.

It is a man. He breaks clear and continues to run but faster now. Here is the Runner – yesterday's runner, breaking clear. But is he hunter or hunted? He runs in pursuit of the silhouette riders who passed through here only moments ago – heading for the plain. The silhouette horsemen – pieces of night on horseback – running with the speed of time – for tomorrow.

The man is being pursued also; he glances back over his shoulder, running headlong out of yesterday. He runs well, fast and strong. It is difficult to believe that anything could stop him, keep pace with him, overtake him. He runs for the plain.

As he becomes surrounded by the emptiness more and more, you can see that he is not alone – single riders, one either side of him, keep pace with him – almost, but not quite out of sight in the distance.

And now another band of horsemen break clear of the forest and they are, apparently, in pursuit of the Runner.

Against the vastness of the plain – the scale sharpens and he is seen to be running at the centre of the riders, a band to the North, one to the South, a single rider each to the East and the West.

The Runner increases his speed but the relationship between him and all the riders remains the same. There is perfect equilibrium. Despite his new speed, nothing changes, the distances are held precisely, minutely.

He runs well but look at his eyes and his fingernails biting deep into the palms of his hands. Look closely and see this man's stress.

He becomes aware of the hill and is tempted to run up its slopes but it is a little out of his path and the running is so important – he feels he must not stop. In fact he pushes on ever harder, runs still faster then tries to run even faster. On and on, he is never happy with the speed he achieves.

The equilibrium is broken when the rider in the East races on ahead of him, taking a diagonal line. The rider slows, turns, in the path of the Runner now. The big horse rears up against the sky, flailing at the twilight with moonlit hooves. But still the Runner runs, dodging past the obstacle almost without seeing it, ignoring it. With thunderous rhythm the Eastern rider gallops on to catch up.

This is the only break in the pattern; the other horsemen maintain the distance exactly as before and nothing it seems could ever break that pattern.

The rider from the East continues to harry the Runner in his attempt at getting him to change course and head for the hill. He cuts in and out and across the path of the man but cannot prevent him from running.

And now the Runner falls. In mid stride, and without apparent warning, he falls and is still. The pall of the unexpected hangs low and heavy around the crumpled figure – and the equilibrium is broken.

There are no riders now to the North, there is no tomorrow. The riders from the South have caught up and have absorbed the horsemen of the West and East. Now they are all together you can see that the Eastern rider is taller and mounted on a larger horse.

They are gathered around the fallen man. Each time the big horse from the East moves in its skittish, stationary dance, a ripple of movement corresponds through all the rest – but freezing now in an unchanging pattern.

The rider looks down on the man.

Jim Perryman is dead.

David Myers
Tuesday

7.09 am

Her eyes were red from crying but the tears were dry now. He could see her lips moving but there seemed to be no sound and then the words registered in his mind.

'There's a cup of tea here, David.'

His thoughts kick started as sleep drained away. He became aware that he was in the lounge, lying on the sofa still wearing his overcoat and the night had left him with a stubbly beard. Caroline was smiling. He cried.

'Oh no, no, *no*!' It all video'd back. He turned away from her in agony, facing the back of the sofa. 'Dear God – no!'

She tried to pull him back to face her but he clung to the confined darkness, burying his head and muffling the sobs which racked him. Eventually, she must have given up and left him there. Eventually, the tears did the same.

His eyes were red from crying but the tears were dry now.

In the kitchen, Caroline was glad to see all the dirty plates and saucepans from last night's meal – they meant something to do, something to cover over the sound of him crying. She squeezed the washing-up liquid into the bowl and watched the hot water swirl up the bubbles. She worked slowly and steadily, concentrating on the task.

Today was Tuesday. She would go shopping later, perhaps get some lamb for dinner. She must remember to get more coffee. Her thoughts were deliberate. They came one after the other like the plates she slotted into the rack. Nice and clean. She had to keep a firm hold on the plates too, in case one of them slipped.

When it was all done, she began to dry them, just as methodically. Within the confines of this action, last night was easier to handle.

. . . . .

David sat up, kicking over the tea she had left him. He watched it soak into the carpet and then let his head sink into his hands.

The smell of bacon came to him and the sound of the kettle coming up to boil – he could hardly believe it. He stood up, took off his overcoat and let it fall untidily on the sofa. The cup lay where he had kicked it. In the mirror above the fire-place he caught sight of a man and went on to the kitchen without any sign of recognition.

She was just putting a plate of bacon and eggs in his usual place. There was the sound of the newspaper falling on the mat. It was like waking up to find that it was yesterday all over again. He scratched at the stubble on his chin and knew it was not.

'Caroline, I want to talk … about last night. …'

She looked at him, impassively then went down the hall to get the paper. He sat down in front of the bacon and eggs, pushing the plate away with revulsion.

She returned. Sitting at her place, she poured a cup of tea and settled down to read.

'I want to talk,' he said, falteringly. 'Don't know what came over me … you see, I …'

She looked up from the paper suddenly, her face showing no sign of any expression.

'I don't want to talk about it.' Her words were flat and final. She paused, as if to be sure her words had been understood, then went back to the paper. He wasn't sure what to do.

A small thought kicking around inside him told him to go upstairs and get ready for work. He ignored it. It wouldn't be that easy.

Her eyes wouldn't focus on the words on the page. It was ironic that he should want to talk and she was stopping him. All the efforts she had made over the years to get him to face up to their problems. David knew all about avoiding the issue. She wondered if he would go upstairs and quietly get ready for work.

'Caroline … I can't bear this. I want to say how sorry I am … I don't know what happened to me.'

She waited to see if he would say any more. There was no more. She kept her eyes on the paper and a rape case came into focus.

'Caroline!' he said insistently. 'I want to *talk*.'

She put the paper down, deliberately.

'How much talking shall we do, David? If we're quick we might just be able to gloss over last night, get the apologies out of the way and send you off to work on time.' There was a core of determination hardening inside her. 'Take a couple of hours off perhaps and we can go back over the last few weeks and months. How many days holiday are you due, David? We could go over it *all*!' Her voice had risen almost to a shout. She wanted to keep control. If she could control her thoughts then surely her voice should be an easy matter?

For the hundredth time since he woke the scene played itself over. Last night he had gone berserk. He dragged her upstairs, slapping and pushing her. Ripping at her clothes in a mad and blind attempt at rape. He couldn't hear her cries at the time but they had filled his head ever since his eyes opened. He had failed to rape her, not because she had proved stronger or because she had escaped, simply because he could not finish what he had started.

Walking, running through the streets for what seemed like most of the night, he had sought refuge from the sickening horror and self-disgust which burned in his stomach.

And now – why was she so calm? Why wasn't she shouting and screaming – wasn't that what he deserved?

When the attempt was over she lay there, still and unmoving, half naked, her clothes torn, not making a sound. He ran.

'I want us to talk,' he said. 'That wasn't me last night; I don't know who it was ... but the thought of it is almost unbearable.'

'Is it?'

He looked at her, horrified.

'What do you mean? Of course it is. ...'

'Of course? What's unbearable, David? The fact that you did it or that you failed?'

The words stung, especially as he didn't know the answer.

'You *know* the answer to that, surely?'

'And, supposing you had succeeded? Wouldn't you have felt just that little better this morning than you do now?'

'Oh this is nonsense. ...'

'For years I've tried to get you to talk this out but you wouldn't. What *is* sex to you?'

'Years! But it's only been a few months since ...' He searched for words.

'Since?'

'Since I haven't been able to ... you know. Everything was perfectly all right before. ...'

80

'You're sure?'

God, she was so calm!

'Yes!' he said firmly. 'Yes it *was*!' He banged his fist on the table, this seemed to be a cue for anger which suddenly flared in her eyes.

'Shall we talk or not! Because *if* we're going to, it'll be *honest*. If not, you might as well clear off to your precious bloody factory. I don't want to hear it!'

All he had really wanted to do was to say sorry. He knew it would never happen again. He just wanted her to realize how sorry he was. He rested his elbows on the table, his head in his hands as he stared vacantly at the settling grease on the bacon and eggs.

She wanted to weaken, looking across at him, his head bowed – she wanted to but they would achieve nothing if she did. It would only increase the anger inside which stemmed not only from the wounding shock and indignation at his treatment of her but also from the implication behind his actions – that it was she alone who was to blame for their sexual problems. The problems were *theirs*, not his or hers and she had been the only one actively trying to solve them – until last night. She could face last night only if something good came from it.

The clock in the lounge chimed 7.30.

'You'd better have a wash and shave; you'll be late for work.' She tested him. He raised his head, glanced at his watch.

'I'm not going in, later perhaps. I don't know.'

She drank some tea and studied him. Somehow she had to prise him open, allowing herself to get angry wasn't going to help.

'How long have we been married?'

'Seventeen years this March.'

'And when was the last time we enjoyed sex? Don't *wince* at the word, it's sex we're talking about.'

'Oh, I don't know,' he said, evasively. 'Three months or four, I can't remember.'

'That was when we had it last. I'm talking about the last time we enjoyed it.'

'I don't know what you're talking about.'

No road in, there.

'How long is it since you were promoted – over Despatch?'

'Look, I don't see ...'

'How long?'

'Two years, six months, three weeks and two days.'

She marvelled at the accuracy then realized what it meant.

'The job was great, to begin with – you remember how keen I was. The department hadn't seen a change in methods for years. I really enjoyed it, got carried away, designing new systems, implementing them – then, later, monitoring success.'

At least he was talking – even if only about work, he was talking.

'And then?'

'Then, one day, it's all done. There are day-to-day problems, sure, but it's all routine. I felt trapped, like I'd achieved all I was going to.'

Then came the disenchantment and the need to reach for a new target. Disenchantment as he watched Henson, Telford and Broughton jockey for position and the new target was promotion. He had felt pretty inadequate next to them and his work began to suffer. He suddenly began to struggle even at the things he was good at. And then there was Caroline at home and the rows and the silence.

'Two and a half years.' She nodded. 'Isn't that about the time things started going wrong here?'

He weighed it, looking for words and a way out. The way things were gathering, it was all his fault. He didn't reply.

'Certainly, the last eighteen months, that's how long sex has been just a Saturday ritual, isn't it? Boring routine – like your job?'

Yes, all his fault. He ignored her words; they made him feel angry and they hurt too much.

'So I went for promotion because I thought that's what *you* wanted. Thought that's what would make you happy.' But the words would not be ignored.

'I thought you were happy – in bed – until very recently. Why did you *pretend*, Caroline, *why*?' He thumped the table again.

'I didn't, David. I never did. You just didn't notice, that's all.' Her words were flat and even, spoken coldly, without emotion and they chilled him.

He felt as if he was gradually being opened up and exposed. He was ashamed of his behaviour last night but probably even more ashamed of his inadequacy over the last few months. Her words were cutting him open.

He swallowed, found nothing to swallow, clenched his hand into a fist. And so it comes to this, he thought, the whole issue, like a sheet of plastic screwed up tight into a ball then released and opening out of its own accord. It didn't matter how tight you made it – it still kept on opening, once you released your grip.

He was studying his fist, watching it unfold. It had been a lie – a small one. In a way she had always pretended but only to a degree. Sex, to her, had always meant giving not receiving. When David was happy she had been. Perhaps it wasn't the way the magazines said but she was genuinely happy and involved when she was giving. But, when it became a ritual, the pretending really started. She began to dread Saturdays and was, of course, unable to talk to him about it, so she stopped acting in the hope this would perhaps alert him to what was happening. It was cruel almost beyond endurance when he didn't even notice, didn't even question it. Last night had almost been easy in comparison. The quiet in the kitchen gnawed at her. She had to keep him talking. She felt remote from him, like a Samaritan talking down a phone line. She *had* to keep him talking.

'I want a divorce.'

He looked up in shock but he said nothing and her anger tightened.

'What am I, David? What *am* I to you? *Answer me!*'

'A divorce? ... but ...?'

As he floundered around in shock her temper ripped loose, pulling words from her tongue as if the accelerator had been jammed on.

'ok! So we're writing this diary of our marriage – let's fill in a few gaps. Seventeen years married. Three years since we last enjoyed sex, maybe? Remember when you were winding yourself up for the last promotion race? How long was it then since we had it? *Five* months! And if you want the weeks and days for your records you can have 'em. And when did we last *talk*, David? I mean really talk like we used to! Talk's like sex isn't it? I mean, you can bang away at it all day and still not have a conversation.' And finally her words were screaming and hysterical. 'For Christ's sake *talk* to me.' And the tears came. 'Where am I?' she cried. 'Where the hell do I *fit* in all this silence?'

His chair scraped on the floor. He went to her, pulling her to her feet – holding her awkwardly. She pushed away from him and ran from

83

the room. He followed. She stood in the lounge, her shoulders moving with the voice of her tears. He stood helplessly behind her.

There was no reaction in him now – in the last few hours it was as if he had been continually hitting a punchball on a tight spring and each time it had jumped back and smacked him in the face. Now the spring had collapsed and the ball lay on the floor. There was nothing to hit, nothing to hit him and no capacity for shock, nothing – except the knowledge that he was standing on a crossroads and all the signs were pointing to the end.

His hands reached out, touching her shoulders. She tensed. His fingers moved to her neck. He tried hard to relax as his finger-tips massaged her skin. She turned into his arms, resting her head on his chest, still crying.

'Perhaps we could go away for a few days,' he said quietly. 'You're so tense – you could relax, we both could.'

Her heart sank with his words and frustration escaped her on the breath of a long, hopeless sigh. It was still all her fault. However subtly he was still shunting all the blame her way.

'No,' she said when she had managed to stop the tears. 'No, we live in this house, within the routine of each day and if we're going to solve it, we'll do it right here – where we've got to live.'

She broke away from him and returned to the kitchen, needing to get away, to think, but he followed. She put the kettle on, avoiding his eyes. She tipped the wasted food into the pedal bin.

'Why don't you go and have a bath?'

He nodded and left. Caroline turned the kettle off before it had boiled and sat down in relief. It would be easy – at any moment things could be set back to the way they were before Monday night – on the surface at least. It was what he was waiting for – it would be easy. Take pretending one stage further, like it never happened. Just sit and wait for the next time. She seemed as far away as ever from getting him to see the problem.

Last night she had come away from the violence full of resolve and determination, to use it to make things better – at least, after the shock had eased, and the fear and the pain had died away – resolve and determination were all she had. Make things better, once and for all, or finish it.

She turned the kettle back on. She had decided to go in hard, as hard as he had last night. If there was a trigger in him somewhere she would find it and make him talk. She was afraid but more afraid of what might happen if things were left as they were. She waited for him.

8.15 am

Sally yawned as she climbed the stairs. The first bin load of letters was ready and waiting for the Order Department to process them. There was almost as much post as on Monday but she had got away to a better start today. It had been strange, arriving at seven with the machines already running. She went into Bette's office with her letters.

'Morning Sally, finished already?'

'No, they're just emptying the order bin but I should be through it all by half past ten.'

'Good.' Bette looked through her letters. 'Let me know as soon as you're ready – I've plenty here waiting.'

Sally smiled as she went to the door.

'Fortunately none of it will involve bending down. I don't think those trousers would stand the strain. Look very smart though – new outfit?'

Sally laughed. 'Yes, I got them Saturday.'

She closed the door. It was a white lie. She bought them some time ago and normally kept them for best. She had nearly made herself late deciding what to wear. Usually she wore her beige blouse with the green trousers and a long crocheted waistcoat – but that covered her bottom. So, eventually, she had decided on wearing a polo-neck jumper under the blouse and tucking them both into the waistband. She felt good and was hopeful that Alan would notice.

She paused outside David Myers's door, knocked and went to go in but it was locked. She raised her eyebrows, shifting his letters to the back of the basket.

Neil Telford was staring out of the window.

'Morning, Mr Telford.' But he made no sign that he had heard her. Again she raised her eyebrows; yesterday he had been chasing her for the mail. She left him, quietly.

She took a deep breath before entering Alan's office. He was on the telephone, doodling on a notepad while he was talking.

'Yes Brian, that's as far as I've got with it. Edgar says he gave it to David to deal with but I'll be seeing David in a moment so I'll let you know. Fine.' He put the phone down.

'Morning, Sally,' he said heavily returning to the figures in front of him.

'Morning,' she said, desperately trying to think of something to say that would make him look up. She put the letters on his desk.

'I couldn't help overhearing . . . Mr Myers isn't in yet, at least, his office is locked.'

He looked up but only to glance at his watch.

'Oh, I expect he will be in a minute,' he said absently. 'Thanks Sally.'

In the corridor a tide of disappointment rillowed all through her but it quickly receded. It was early yet.

When she went into Edgar Broughton's office he too was studying a page of figures but he looked up as she walked towards him. She could feel his eyes on her but avoided looking at him. She left, half wishing she had worn the waistcoat after all.

8.25 am

There was no getting clear of it. If he could just pull clear he would make it up to her but there was a determination about her he had never seen before.

He dressed, feeling slightly better. There were things she didn't realize. She was hauling him in like a fish on the line without knowing what she had caught. But he couldn't put up the shutters, he would lose her then, as surely as he would lose her if she persisted.

He looked at his watch – it had stopped – he didn't bother to wind it. What did it matter?

Divorce. They had come all down the road, on to the crossroads, to face that. Did that road really stretch back three years or more? If he could only get clear, past Christmas, things would be better then, she'd *see*.

It seemed true but he knew it wasn't, deep down he knew. This wasn't taking the pattern of their usual rows. She wasn't nagging at him on the surface; she was probing, deeper and deeper.

He finished dressing and went downstairs. The clock in the lounge chimed the half-hour.

'Feel any better?' He certainly looked it. He nodded. She watched him steadily as he sat down. The table was now completely cleared and they sat at opposite ends.

'Where to now?' she asked.

'I want to try and pick up the pieces – carry on. Couldn't bear a divorce ... couldn't.'

He was talking slowly, measuring his words and he was staring at the pattern on the table, avoiding her eyes.

'After last night, I'm not sure if we can.'

He went to protest, but she carried on. 'How do you think I feel? Supposing it happens again? Do you think I want to live with that fear – half fear – always there?'

'Oh look!' he said, exasperated, animated at last. 'Don't be so silly, last night was ...'

'*Silly*?' The edge she put on the word stopped him. 'Can't you see? That wasn't just me you were pushing around last night, it was the trust between us. Where is it now? I'm not going to become a battered wife, David – no chance.'

'Last night was ...' He brought his words out so deliberately, obviously gripping hard on a growing rage. She felt a stab of fear in her stomach but couldn't stop now.

'OK – last night – come on then, what *was* last night?' she goaded.

'It was pressure. I snapped, OK? It was intolerable pressure. I'd give anything to go back and make it like it never happened!'

'I see and that's the way you see it, is it? One hundred per cent. No other thoughts on the matter? No doubts?'

'God, Caroline! I can't *do* any more. I can't go back and undo it. It was vile and I'm sorry for it. It *won't* happen again. What more can I say?'

'A damned sight more, believe me, if there are going to be any pieces picked up!' She snapped back, then she calmed her voice. 'So. This theory of yours – about pressure – let's look at it. Seems reasonable enough. Quite normal behaviour, must happen all the time. Husband, trying to cope with a floundering career and the half chance of promotion, loses sexual drive. Can't just accept that.

Can't see that stress and over-work and sex can't always be forced into the same bed. No. Solution? Husband goes home and beats up the little woman...'

'Caroline!'

'... beats up the little woman but can't quite rape her. Male ego even more dented, better luck next time? Wallowing in self pity next day he pleads with the little woman, wants her to help him pick up the pieces – the ones *he* smashed. Why the hell should I? You bloody *enjoyed* it – I saw you!'

He leapt from the chair, his face twisted into the same expression it wore last night. He came for her, fists clenched. She gritted her teeth, kept her hands on the table, made no motion to defend herself. He checked, turning on his heel.

'Go on then!' she screamed after him. 'Run, you bastard – RUN!'

He ran. The front door slammed with a force that seemed to shake the entire house. Caroline sat trembling – in silence.

A squashed up car distorted its way across the frosted glass of the front door. He tried to stare through the glass, his hands still clenched into fists. The words in his mind which had stopped him on the threshold still lingered – go now and you'll never get back in. And he had slammed the door and it was still slamming in his head with as much force as if he had been beating his head against the woodwork. He returned to the kitchen.

Caroline watched dispassionately as he sat down. He had a hunted, desperate look and his eyes would not meet hers. She felt like a camera, just watching, a spectator.

When he ran from the kitchen and her words still hung across the gulf between them, she had continued to stare at the empty door-way thinking that it was all beyond her control. It could do as it pleased; it could end if it wanted to; it could begin again – if it wanted to.

She watched him. His hands were on the table. His suit gave him an incongruous air of efficiency – but ... His face, the barriers were down – at least partly. The lines on his brow, his eyes – restless, hands too. Strange, she found herself thinking, you cannot choose who you love, it's just something that is.

'Funny how you lose it, isn't it?' he said quietly, his eyes still avoiding her. 'I mean, you don't look back, no need, and you don't look forwards, no more than you have to. And there you are, looking at the bit in front of you.'

She was puzzled by his words and his voice had changed, somehow. Its tone was less – she searched for the word – less formal.

'It's not fixed or anything; get yourself into rough waters and it can shrink down from the next couple of weeks, say, down to a matter of hours and minutes, seconds even – like now. But it doesn't really matter how far ahead that bit is – well, to most of you it does, but to one small part it doesn't, and that's the part that gets you through, d'you see? It gets people through wars; it got you through last night. It's the part that's programmed to do just that – get you through. Understand?'

She didn't, quite, but it was reassuring to hear him talk; it was a luxury.

'Go on,' she said.

He wasn't thinking about what he was saying any more – the words were just coming and he was listening almost as intently as Caroline.

'Sometimes, you see, it can get itself locked on – fixed and you get so you can't see more than one step ahead – you know? No idea of direction any more, just that next step and you're travelling so fast because of it, can't see, can't listen, no perspective, just travel on through it.'

He paused, almost out of breath but there was no stopping. It had to be all or nothing now if he was going to tell her at all. He had tried to pull clear with as little said as possible. She had prevented him.

'Have you stopped travelling now?' The harshness had gone from her voice. He looked away.

'I'm not sure, just as you don't see it when it starts to happen to you, you're not aware of it. I think so. I'm not sure. It's like waking up and remembering a dream, a nightmare – only to find that it actually happened and you're stuck with it.'

She reached across the table for his hand: he dodged it.

'By Saturday I suppose I'd got to the point where I wasn't seeing anything any more. I was living piecemeal, a bit at a time. Get this done, move on to the next thing. Sex on Saturday. Great. That's that out of the way for another week. But then it refused to be crossed off the list. It stopped. And at work, the usual Christmas lunacy only I'm not coping like I used to. Promotion and all the back biting and the worry about Saturday travels into work with you. And every-where they're all talking about it, joking about it – sex – and I feel so, ashamed because I know how they'd laugh if they knew. Nothing funnier nor so rich in comedy as incompetence and impotence.'

His fists clenched now on the table and his words spilling even faster.

'The worry about sex, it goes to work with you and the pressure comes home with you and you try to keep it out but it doesn't hide in the briefcase that you bring home, it slips past that door in your head.' He paused, abruptly. 'And then there was Saturday – another row and I stormed out of the house – remember? I drove around not knowing what was really going on and she was walking along by the Town Hall, looking upset. So I offered her a lift, just so I wouldn't be alone, any more. I offered her a lift...'

She tensed up again. The thought that there might be someone else had always plagued her and when sex had stopped completely she became sure of it – almost. Unable to help herself, the green streak of jealousy and envy had laced its way through the colour of their rows. She knew what he meant about people and their endless talk of sex. Her problems and David's had alienated her from some of the conversations her friends indulged in, though she tried hard not to show it. When Caroline had ventured to talk to one of them about it, she had made it all so simple. 'Obvious,' she had said, 'He's got someone else – you do the same – easy, why not?' It was only the 'why not' that was easy – because she still loved David.

'Who is it?' she said across what he was saying and her voice was cold.

9.05 am

Sally watched as her hands skimmed the letters into the bin, darting out to the pigeon-holes. In the wake of disappointment because Alan hadn't noticed her, guilt came back. It was wrong, she knew it was hopeless but without the feeling which had flared up, what was there? Only the hurt because Gary had finally ditched her and the fear and shock still vibrating since Saturday.

If it had been Edgar Broughton or Neil Telford she never would

90

have accepted the lift – she had heard enough stories from the other girls to know what they were like. She had felt safe and, when they were talking, it had seemed all right, even though she couldn't tell him what was really on her mind. He was very understanding until it all went wrong.... She shook away the thoughts.

''lo, Sal. How's it going? Like the trousers. God, I feel awful. I'm never drinking again, definitely not before the next time....'

She watched her hands work, for once Angela's voice was very welcome.

9.10 am

'No, Caroline. It isn't the "someone else" you've always expected to appear. She doesn't exist and never has. Sally's just a girl at work, a really nice kid. She was very upset and I stopped the car. We were talking. I listened to her problems and they seemed so small but then I matched them against mine when I was seventeen or eighteen and they seemed pretty big then.'

He could feel her tensing up again but there was no stopping.

'Things were getting her down. Her brother keeps telling her she's ugly. Her boyfriend had just stood her up. No one to talk to at work. She didn't seem to have any confidence in herself. I was really shocked. I mean, she's so bright at the office. She's such a good-looking girl. I think I may have laughed at the idea of her thinking she's ugly but stopped myself. I could see it hurt and remembered what it's like when someone laughs your biggest fears away. I tried to kiss her. Oh no – no excuses...' He held his hands up in surrender. 'There was no "come on" from her, she's very naïve really, innocent almost. I wasn't thinking straight – God, when did I last do that? I kissed her because it seemed like an answer – to show her how attractive she is. Yes, sounds so silly now – sounds really good doesn't it? But I kissed her and got excited, wouldn't let her push me away....'

'You didn't...' Her voice, strained and tight, jumped into the line of his words.

'No, I didn't rape her.' It was natural for her to think it after Monday – but it hurt all the same. 'But I did get carried away, a bit frenzied. It scared her, scared her badly but I was *excited, aroused* –

after all that time ... ah but, no excuses. She was struggling and I suddenly realized what the hell I was doing. All this in seconds, just seconds. She got out and ran and I sat there for, oh, couple of hours I suppose. Couldn't believe it; couldn't accept those few seconds. By the time I got back here I actually *didn't* believe it. Everything shut down, all inside. Staring at that bit in front and nothing else.'

Poor Sally, she thought, but at least there was no real harm done. If she was as innocent as David said then it was better someone like him, perhaps she'd be more wary. He wasn't a predator – she had met those before getting married – and even since. 'No' isn't an answer, it's an encouragement.

She had relaxed, sitting there listening to him, watching him. She knew he was being honest, sensed it. It would have been easy to blame Sally, lessen his part, perhaps suggest encouragement on her part followed by cold feet.

It was the first time he had talked about sex or anything related without the usual game of hide-and-seek. Whenever it came up before there had always been the reserve in his eyes or he would evade the subject, ducking into the accepted innuendo and never getting any further.

'That was on Saturday,' she said. 'What happened on Monday?'

There was silence. She got up suddenly. He looked startled. She turned the kettle on, put two cups on the table.

'Come on, love,' she said gently. 'We've got pieces to pick up.'

He smiled, faintly.

All the weeks gone past – he saw them. Days, running on slippery, hard-packed snow with him pushing a bobsleigh, jumping in and blurring down through the week. Steep Saturday turns and wall of death Sundays twisting you straight out into Monday and on and on, down through the week. But yesterday refused to be Monday.

He listened to his words, watched them in-ing and out-ing the images, missing the picture. Monday had been a day of distorted images. Seeing Sally when she brought the post and wanting and wanting and wanting to say sorry but the words not being able to escape. She had left hurriedly and then Alan had brought the crisis through his door.

Distorted images, like being trapped in a hall of mirrors only it isn't funny any more. Voices all whispering out at him, advising and urging him.

It works with Sally – why not Caroline? Why the big deal anyway? Quick grope in the car, that was all. Can't you hear them laughing? Edgar and Neil. What would Edgar think? Laugh himself silly, that's all. He had seen Edgar operate, caught him at it and he'd been only too pleased to explain the rules of his little game. She'd know worse, probably had known worse. When did you change your name to Broughton, David?

Questions and voices, layered on top of one another and overlapping. It's ok! For God's sake, man, go home and put your arms round Caroline, give her a kiss and no problem.... But don't fail this time, another warned, all or nothing stakes, can't take another failure....

Too many failures, weeks and months of them stacked up in neat rows. 'Ah, but if you were a *man* ...' a voice overlapped and swirled down the aisles of the warehouse where his failures were stored and inventoried '... this whole thing would soon be settled.'

Remember the night she came into the lounge wearing her house-coat, how she let it fall open and she was wearing all that sexy underwear? Stockings and suspenders? Remember how pleased you were – and how you failed, even then? Remember being crushed by the look of failure in *her* eyes. Now if you were a *man* ...

And on and on the insane voices babbled out their closed up words, jet streaming into one another, voice on top of voice throughout the day. All those words swimming around like bacteria, in and out of the figures on his desk – adding up.

He tried to get the words to fit the pictures.

She listened intently; his words were confused and mixed up; there was no stopping them. She sometimes glimpsed, behind the confusion, scenes of great clarity and these she understood. She saw the tender, raw innocence of a boy who had never grown up in relation to women. Who had probably never spoken to anyone – male or female – as he was speaking now, and, for him, that was a lot.

'I'm not sure if you can understand....' he said.

'I think I can,' she interrupted. 'Let me try. It's Monday night, we're watching TV in silence, as usual, and it's getting near bed-time and it's all up there in your head – yes? Your ego is practically non-existent, even the minute success with Sally is covered in shame. There's the tension between us, your dented confidence at work and you just don't know how to begin. Sex has grown out of proportion and into obsession and you can't talk about it. Your pride stops you from even reaching out and touching me. You want to begin – to try – but dare not fail, because of the consequences. Suddenly – SNAP – violence, get it over, one way or another – get it over. And getting it over wasn't so very different from the Saturday ritual, was it?'

He nodded. 'I'm sorry, love,' he said, 'I'm sorry.'

'But do you understand, David? Can you see why it happened?'

'No, if I could see I might have been able to stop it.'

'Maybe if we could start treating one another like people again. You treated Sally like a person, until it went wrong, and you got a response. You're going for promotion but you don't *have* to. You don't really want it, I don't. I want us. Sex isn't something that has to be had because the clock says it's time. All those Saturdays – you weren't enjoying it any more than I was – is it any wonder your body says, no thanks, can't see the point of this.'

He smiled. She got up and put her arms round his neck. He drew her to him, his head resting against her.

'There *is* no point,' she said ruffling his hair. 'Feeding an ego, it can't be done, too hungry. Once it's big enough, it'll eat you. Monday wasn't so different to the ritual, you know – you dominating in a violent sense rather than a physical one, needing to maintain that ego more than physically needing the sex, do you see?'

'Yes, I think so ...'

'And now – go to work,' she said firmly, breaking away from him. 'Tell Sally how sorry you are, don't be afraid.'

'But, we can't leave it here, like this....'

'We're not, though, are we? Work is part of it. We've cleared the tension; we'll carry on tonight, and tomorrow and next month – we'll do it within the framework of our lives. Go to work; do the job you're good at, forget promotion.'

He nodded slowly.

'And when we're clear of all this, we'll take a holiday!' she said brightly. 'We can enjoy it then.'

He smiled again. It masked the strain and the tension still there in his face, but it was a smile.

'OK I'll go but ...' it faded '... I know I shan't be able to get away at five. It's a madhouse there love, in the middle of a crisis. You don't know what it's like ...'

'I understand,' she said. 'It's not just you they load the pressure on to, love, it's all of us. I was talking to Nancy Henson the other day ... Anyway, enough talking now – more tonight – yes? About seven or eight?'

He got up, kissed her. 'Sooner if I can. Bye.'

There was a parking meter free outside the library. David stopped the car, impulsively and reversed into the gap. His spirits were rising with each passing minute. There is *never* a free meter outside the library, he thought as he locked the car. He went into the building and found a spare table to sit at. He was unwilling to go to work – yet. Reaching for a leaflet, he pretended to read. The hush of the library settled on him. There were millions of words all around him but hardly any inside and he could hardly believe it. When his thoughts did begin to pick up, they were calm and easy. It was Tuesday. A sixty per cent increase was at that moment on its way through to his department but at the end of the day there was Caroline. He would make it up to her; he was determined.

He glanced at the clock on the wall and began to wind his watch.

11.14 am

As she walked past the open door, Alan was searching for the right key. Bette looked on as he tried to open David Myers's desk then looked round.

'Ah Sally, don't go. You can take these keys back to the lodge in a moment.'

'Got it!' Alan said. Sally went in. Alan began to open the drawers and his expression of triumph faded into one of shock.

'Bloody hell,' he said, glancing at Bette. She looked surprised too. Natural curiosity drew Sally further into the office. The drawers of the desk were overflowing with a chaos of paper; some were difficult to open they were so full. The papers, letters, photostats and figures were crammed and crumpled into the drawers without regard for them being creased, screwed up or even torn.

Several moments passed as they stood there, held by the odd and

95

unexpected sight in the almost painfully tidy room. She saw their expressions change as they both looked beyond her. She felt someone brush past.

'Morning, David,' Alan said guiltily. 'Had to get the pass key I'm afraid; it's this McKenzie thing Brian is flapping over. . . .' He moved away from the desk, out of David's way.

As he turned Sally saw his face. She glimpsed for a second what she thought he would look like in ten or fifteen years' time. He seemed so old and so tired as he stared down at the drawers gaping open.

He smiled, calmly.

'McKenzie? That rings a bell, let me see, now . . .' He sat down and began to scoop the papers out on to the desk. 'Yes, here we are!' He produced a crumpled letter and smoothed it out flat on the desk, then he read it as if for the first time.

'Mm. Think you had better deal with it, Alan. None of these in stock.'

Alan took the letter from him raising his eyes to the ceiling in exasperation but he said nothing and left.

'Now. I wonder if I could just have a word with Sally, Bette?' Sally's heart sank.

'Yes, fine. Perhaps you'd give her the keys,' she said as she left.

She felt shut in when the door closed and moved slightly away from the desk.

'No, don't run away; you were right to on Saturday, not today, please.'

She felt a little reassured by the faint sadness in his tone. She didn't trust it.

11.16 am

'I'm sorry, desperately sorry for what happened. I can't explain. I can't tell you how sorry . . . It happened and I didn't mean it to . . .'

'Well, I think perhaps we ought to . . .' She sounded so nervous.

'Forget it? Wish I could. Please Sally, believe me . . . I didn't mean to frighten you.'

'It's OK.' She shrugged as if wishing to make light of it.

'It isn't, I know that. Don't ever let it be. Just know that I'm sorry

96

and that you don't need to feel – threatened or afraid, or anything – OK?'

She nodded, managing to smile, just. He watched her leave aware of her relief in doing so. His eyes returned to the untidy papers on his desk, a screwed up memo reflected perfectly in its shine. He allowed all the filtered noises to absorb into him as he looked on. Footsteps. A telephone ringing persistently somewhere. A heavy lorry trying to manoeuvre up to the loading bay outside and, in every beam and shadow of the building, the rhythm and drone of the machines.

No more reflections. He began to empty out the rest of the drawers until there was no more room on the desk top for reflections. Spent leaves of a calendar. Things he had meant to action, evaluate, look at over the last few weeks. It was surprising how long things could be left to run before something bit back at you.

He was working steadily through it all when Bette came in. He smiled.

'Spring cleaning?'

He laughed and motioned for her to sit down.

'I didn't phone this morning,' she said. 'I guessed you'd either come in later or phone but I thought you'd like a bit of help so I took the liberty ...' She sorted through the file on her lap. 'Here's a breakdown of current order levels, average order size; complete breakdown of carton stocks and materials – current and obsolete.'

He looked at her in admiration as, with each item, she handed him a sheet of paper.

'List of materials scheduled for delivery this week and next; copies of contracts we have with the private post firms, in case you need them and ...' she handed him a final sheet. '... an up to date stock check as at nine-forty-five.'

He grinned. Their relationship had always been a little strained before now, mainly because he didn't quite approve of career women but also because her obvious efficiency made him want to catch her out.

'You've been busy,' he said not hiding his surprise or appreciation.

'I wasn't surprised when you didn't arrive this morning,' she said quietly. 'You looked in a bad way when you left here last night and I thought it best to hang on a bit before phoning. Don't thank me for all that.' She nodded at the papers he was collecting into a tidy sheaf.

97

'Thank your team; they did all the work, all I did was ask. They're good, aren't they?'

'Not bad. Not bad at all. Bette this is great. Don't know how to thank you.'

She waved the words aside, smiling.

'You seem better this morning – don't look it – but I'm glad you're getting things sorted.' Again she nodded, this time at the clutter on his desk and he returned her smile as she got up to leave.

'Thanks, Bette, mean that.'

She closed the door and his watch said 11.35.

12.35 pm

'Ah! Edgar. I've got a lot of left-over stock from last Christmas. There's a list in my office.'

Edgar continued to feed the coffee machine with money.

'Well,' he said evasively, 'I'm a bit tied up at the moment . . .'

'Yes, me too, but it won't take a moment.' David wasn't going to be put off. They walked down the corridor to his office.

Edgar raised an eyebrow when he saw the untidy desk.

'Your salesmen can't be doing much now; they can load up their cars and flog it off next week.' He handed the list to Edgar who nodded slowly as he read through it. 'I need the space.'

Edgar sat down and sipped at his coffee. David groaned inwardly; far from being busy Edgar seemed to have all the time in the world.

'Yes, all right then. Get it packed and I'll circularize a memo. . . .'

'It's packed already and I need the rack space now, so perhaps you could phone round.'

'Mm. See what I can do,' Edgar said, disinterested. 'Are you getting enough stock through from Henson?'

'Yes, Edgar.' David was becoming annoyed. 'But there'll be nowhere to put it if I don't clear some space.' Edgar was just hunting for ammunition. He seemed unusually vague, as if his mind was elsewhere.

'Cut it a bit fine this year didn't you Edgar? It's touch and go – we may not get this work out in time.'

'Every confidence, old chap. I did a quick tour of the sales

98

territories, whipping up a bit of enthusiasm. It's going to finish up a good year – a good run, late on. Have you seen Neil this morning? Wandering around like a lost soul. Still, having lunch with him in a minute so I'll soon find out what's wrong.'

'Fine. You do that. Now, if you don't mind ...'

Edgar got up, drinking the last of his coffee.

'Don't forget the list.'

'Ah, knew I'd forgotten something, thanks.'

David sighed when he had gone. He didn't relish the thought that it might be Edgar who won promotion. He was good at his job, maybe that gave him the time to be so political in his approach. He would never be able to resist grinding away at Henson. It was bad enough at present. Surely Brian could see that? Maybe it would be Neil but, in his own way, he was just another Edgar, very political, sharp and astute but his motives were often questionable. Like Alan, he could be a little short-sighted. Who then? Not me, he thought, too conservative. The firm was itching for expansion, needed someone willing to take risks – the right ones and at the same time motivate the good but difficult team at his disposal. David had always wanted to be an important, vital member of a team, but not the captain. Brian had probably given him Despatch for that reason.

David pulled his thoughts away from promotion. There was work to do, though it was nice to look at it objectively now.

Bette popped her head round the door.

'Treat you to lunch if you like.'

He smiled.

'Thanks but I've got some catching up to do.'

She nodded.

'See you later then.'

Bette's quiet and unobtrusive support was welcome and unexpected. Perhaps it was always there, he thought, waiting for a response. Catching up to do, his own words echoed in his head and he reached for the telephone.

3.55 pm

'Yes. I know how difficult it is . . .' he said into the telephone. The fingers of his free hand were crossed. 'Deliver to us tomorrow and I promise you a big order next year. All right then Thursday, latest. Mm. Yes, I imagine you will need a night shift; we've got one.' David listened, his eyes fixed on the picture on the wall. 'Fine, it's a deal.' He grinned. 'Thursday latest, remember. I'll confirm in writing. Bye.'

He rang off and uncrossed his fingers. He had just managed to get more cartons delivered. It wasn't enough but it was better than nothing. He let his gaze remain on the picture a moment. A soft, gentle scene, mist rising over a marshland but it was the sky that held him. It had a perspective all its own, a three-dimensional sense of vastness, unending until the tree tops pulled you back into the real perspective.

He smiled at his success on the phone. It wasn't enough, they would still be short. He reached for the list Bette had given him of obsolete carton stocks; the figures were going to prove invaluable.

When it all began to start up again, the crisis and the deadline pressing in, he moved with it, was carried along. It was as if he had actually been thinking about it all the while. Searching across a seemingly endless waveband for a lost radio station but now he had found it, the static and interference cleared.

Everything was running smoothly again. Now, if he could just find a use for these cartons. . . .

7.21 pm

David stopped, sat back in the chair and rubbed his eyes. He knew he had passed the point of tiredness which prevented him from being effective. He yawned. He was ravenous; there hadn't been time to eat anything.

But there was the quiet satisfaction inside; he knew he had caught up with the crisis and overtaken it perhaps. By the time he started work again in the morning it would have edged ahead again. Another day, closer to the deadline, less time, travelling faster. But he was satisfied.

Automatically he began to tidy his desk but then decided to leave it. He put his coat on wearily, looking forward to seeing Caroline, hardly able to believe the time had passed so quickly.

There was a slight doubt in his mind though. He still could not afford to fail if she felt the time was right to make love. Fear threatened to re-emerge from beneath the doubt but he pressed it down hard. Everything was running smoothly again. He turned out the light and slammed the door behind him.

The picture on the wall tilted slightly off line and there was the sound of his footsteps disappearing hurriedly down the corridor.

Tuesday Night

11.55 pm

Neil watched the numbers change. The digital clock, with its tiny green aura fending off the dark, continued to pin-point the seconds and underline the time.

He had got through the day without thinking of her. The shock of her death lay somewhere in his mind, unmoving all day, now it stirred and stood between him and sleep.

Angela had been difficult to shake off but he had managed it somehow. It didn't matter that he had been forced to hurt her in the process. She crowded him with her voice and her wanting to make amends. Her attitude seemed to have changed. She appeared to have adopted an almost motherly, protective stance towards him. Had she woken? Heard him crying?

He didn't want to know. He might have kicked her, the way she reacted to his sharp words. But she had left him alone and Judi was somewhere in the North out of reach and Jenny was dead.

He turned on his side and let his mind pick up the familiar, brightly coloured threads of his daydreams. The way things would be if tomorrow was perfect. The perfect day. Ever since childhood he had played the game whilst waiting for sleep to come. Tomorrow there would be someone or something; the great empty space in his life would be filled. He sometimes felt like the centre of a maze, hollow and bare, trapped there in the centre waiting for someone or something to find a way through. Sometimes he wanted to shout out loud, to help them, but he could not.

He turned back over and the clock watched him, silently.

Sally leant on the window sill looking out at the cloud troubled moon, her dressing-gown drawn tightly around her against the cold. Every few minutes she had to wipe her breath from the glass and each time her thoughts would start afresh.

Gary had called at the house but she had been working late. He phoned her at the factory, apologetic, genuinely sorry because he had stood her up on Saturday but he wouldn't say why. He said he had done a lot of thinking and wanted to talk. She wasn't sure what to say and tried to get out of a meeting but he insisted, seeming so upset and sad and so ... young, somehow.

Saturday seemed far away. She felt a long way from the girl waiting beneath the Town Hall clock. She agreed eventually to meet him tomorrow night, but now she wasn't sure.

She wiped the glass and watched a straggly looking dog nose idly under a hedge before moving on, disappointed.

Gary had sounded different. It was obviously important to him that he see her. She was flattered, had weakened but worried now if she had done the right thing. Alan might want her to work late. Perhaps she had agreed just to give herself an opportunity to stand him up – but that would be mean and she knew she would probably go. It would get rid of him though. He would be too proud to ring again.

She wiped the glass again, angrily, annoyed at the endless confusion inside her. She didn't *want* to be rid of him. The moon was beginning to fold away behind the clouds, bit by bit. She took off her dressing-gown and crept into bed, shivering. She curled up into a ball and hoped she would dream of Alan.

David felt safe and secure in her arms and sleep was coming. There was only the sound of her heartbeat and the night-time sounds outside. She stroked his hair.

It was almost as if they had just met, talking and talking through what was left of the evening when he got home. Throughout the meal and the washing up, just talking, and when it was all cleared away he held her and they kissed. He did it because he wanted to; it seemed natural but his fear had tightened up again, tugging at him like a dog on a lead, pulling him back.

Maybe she had sensed it. When the kiss was over she had slipped off her wedding ring and put it on the draining board. No sex, she had said, reassuringly with a teasing, seductive smile. No kissing or intimate touching either. Tomorrow perhaps, they could touch, or the day after. Later they could kiss and touch. It was a game. One day they would be able to make love again and they would both know when that day should be. He had tried to hide his relief but

103

made no effort to conceal his interest. Sex was something to look forward to again, something of value.

He heard the sound of footsteps running outside. Her hand stopped stroking him a moment and then resumed as the footsteps passed on and down the street. He followed them into the dark and continued his journey down the sleepy, velvet lined road that would lead him out into morning.

'It's got to stop, Alan! Why won't you *listen?*'

He could feel her getting into bed but didn't turn round to face her.

'Listen,' she said, poking him gently in the back. 'It was after ten again when you got home. You look dreadful and you hardly touched your supper.'

He turned over, smiling.

'I'll tickle you.'

'Oh come on, Alan, this is serious.'

But he couldn't let it be.

'All this nonsense people talk,' he moaned, trying to mask the smile. 'Food! I mean, who needs it? Sleep? Just details, love – nobody really needs these things; it's just habit, social custom. I'll get figures. Prove it.'

'Idiot!' She smiled.

'Don't keep on at me, love. Must sleep. It's only for this week, all these hours, promise. Must keep going,' he said drowsily, eyes closing. 'This is an official sleep period, not a talk period, or a row period or an anything period except sleep.'

She turned out the light and sighed, snuggling up to him. He hadn't told her the alarm was set for 5.30. The darkness hit him at the same time sleep did.

There was a prickly, uncomfortable feeling between his shoulder blades. It had been there, vaguely, all day. Edgar had brought it out of sleep – this niggling feeling that something was wrong. His mind trawled its nets through the past few days – but the waters were over-fished. He'd been over it so many times. The nets kept coming in empty and the feeling persisted and grew. Everything he could think of had been checked. He had back tracked through recent files, even those not so recent.

He lay in bed and let his eyes sort out the darkness. This was his waking nightmare – to overlook something, something important – the feeling between his shoulders was an infallible early warning. Illogically, strangely, his thoughts kept leading him back to the list of visitors. He shied from the thought like a frightened horse. Nothing there, it couldn't be that causing the feeling, nothing there.

As far as he could tell, he was out in the clear. He had fixed the sales projection and smoothed over some tricky wave-making from Brian. Anyway, Brian seemed more concerned about the McKenzie letter than anything else. Plenty of meat still to be picked from that bone.

Where was the danger? Henson? He would crack; he was teetering right there on the edge. Myers? He was never in the race; the fact that he missed Brian's phone round up and that the letter had ended up on his desk when the music stopped had merely confirmed it. Neil? He was so quiet at lunch. Edgar had felt a little sorry for him and greatly surprised. In some ways it was like looking at himself when he had been in his thirties. Dealing with Neil, it was almost unfair. Bette then? He dismissed it. Where then?

Nowhere. He was out in the clear. The thought tried to reassure him and the feeling kept making him glance over his shoulder to see if the tracks he wanted to be covered were indeed hidden.

Out in front. He turned on his side and searched for sleep. He tried to reach between his shoulder blades; exasperated he turned back and gazed up at the ceiling.

Listen to me. Hear the clock beating out the time. Time is running. Fast and slow, at so many different tempos and all at the same speed. You chase after it. Where are you running from? Away from yesterday. Where to? Into tomorrow.

Look at the scene again. Can you see it? It looks the same. The tangled forest, the empty plain, this hill top. But it's another forest and you've come here again.

There are the horsemen, breaking out across the plain: there you are – in pursuit – the Runner, looking over your shoulder, running just ahead of exhaustion. The riders from the South pursue. To the East, to the West, the single riders. The balance is the same, the equilibrium perfect, no matter how fast, how slow you run, no matter what.

And there's this hill. You see it, tempted to climb it. Climb it. But that would slow you down, wouldn't it? That's the very idea – the hill always arrives at the exact moment in your life when you have enough, just enough, in reserve to scale it, no more. It's a last chance.

The Eastern rider is breaking formation. See? He tries to get you in the way of it so that you have to climb it. He rears up in front of you but you won't listen. The world is just a blurred vibration because your steps are so heavy now, they jolt you. You can choose to run on, past the hill, use up the last of you by running on. It's your choice. There is time. All of time is yours: all the time you have is yours.

I can stop you. I will. That's the only thing which is definite. I'm going to stop you. Despite all my warnings, it will hit you hard. Shock. Can you withstand it? Jim Perryman couldn't.

Run on then, but you won't make it to Friday no matter how fast you run. Listen to me. Watch this scene closely, there are things you can see from up here you can't see when you're running. Watch.

The time is running down midnight. Watch. There is one horseman in the band to the North, his horse is turning lame – see? Now it is moving slowly enough for you to catch him up. Those Northern riders, you can catch them only one at a time. You can destroy them all if you do not take heed but you can only catch them one by one.

You're drawing closer to the Northern horse now. Look to the West, he's lame too, that's why you kept pace with him, why he kept pace with you. Only you can set the pace.

Now you're coming through midnight. It is the turn of the day and as it slips past you the Northern horse is moving out to the West. Now it is level with you, running with you. The horse from the West has fallen back, has joined those to the South – behind you now, the equilibrium is restored. Now there is one less ahead of you, one more behind you.

It's another day. Do you see? It's all so simple. I'll run it again. . . .

Edgar Broughton
Wednesday

6.45 am

It wasn't hard for Edgar – getting out of bed; it was almost a relief. He slipped by the opening routines of the day unnoticed. He washed, selected his third suit of the week, a freshly laundered shirt. He skimmed through breakfast, the morning paper and the usual conversation with his sister. He felt desperately tired but that was nothing new – there was a day to be faced. He skimmed through the car radio news and the familiar drive to the factory, a nagging tightness in his chest, the feeling still there between his shoulders, still out of reach.

But he did not skim through the papers on his desk or in his files. Despite the controlled care as he checked and rechecked everything, he could find nothing. Everything was as it should be, it seemed. He was out in front.

Restlessness pulled him from his desk and took him to the window, abandoning his preparations for Friday's meeting. He leaned on the window sill, his chin resting on his hands. He gazed out at the windswept car-park. Beneath the dark, his car was parked next to Henson's. His mind followed an endless search pattern and kept alighting momentarily on the list of visitors' names. This further annoyed him and a new pattern was started.

Alan's words came back to him. 'Have you withdrawn the range?' How many times had he checked the files since then? Yes – the memo had gone out, the catalogues been withdrawn. He had even checked, discreetly, with three of the most reliable members of his team. Everything was fine. Why was demand so high then? To begin with he had put it down to the whirlwind tour he had made, concentrating on his newer salesmen, urging them on. Push, push, push. He needed the sales. They had already given him a good set of figures but good wasn't good enough – he wanted brilliant. To clinch promotion nothing less would do. This was his last chance, he sensed that but he also sensed that his motivation alone would not have produced the increase even though he had told his men quietly to push right up to the deadline and a little beyond it. Production would cope.

It was all locked up so tight and yet he would have put money on this area being the cause of his concern. Something was wrong, somewhere....

'Morning, Edgar.'

He straightened up abruptly, wincing as he turned from the window, rubbing his back.

'Morning, Brian,' he said, recovering and regretting that he had been caught in such an uncharacteristic pose. 'Have a seat. I didn't see your car.'

'Having back trouble? Old age catching up on you, eh?' Brian was smiling but there was no laughter in his eyes, there rarely was.

'Too quick for that,' he replied, laughing, resenting the implication. They sat down.

Looking at Brian it was difficult to believe he was only forty-one; occasionally he looked younger but Edgar thought most people would put him as the younger man. Edgar envied him his age as well as his job.

'My car's in dock – again,' Brian was saying. 'I came by taxi. I'll use our spare now I'm here. Still, I'm glad we have this chance for a chat. Things might get a bit hairy later.'

Promotion. The word switched on in neon lights.

'So, what's going on, Edgar?'

He was slightly disconcerted by the firmness of the question; it was almost accusatory but, inside, he was buzzing and alive. The lights were flashing in blues and purples. He gushed a little in reply, going over the speech he had rehearsed, stressing how far ahead he was. A curt wave of the hand and the exasperated frown which Brian always wore when things were not as he wanted them, stopped him in mid sentence.

'No, no. Save all that for the meeting. I'm talking about sales projection figures that aren't delivered, sales way above budget forcing us into a very expensive two shift situation.'

The lights were dimmed somewhat.

'I see.' Edgar nodded knowingly. 'Henson has been bleating has he? All I know is that he got the figures on Thursday – a day late, damn it. Yours weren't delivered because of a stupid oversight by the post-girl.' He spread his hands wide and shrugged. 'Unfortunate, but – it happens. We're all under pressure here, Brian. I don't want to knock Alan's efforts but, quite honestly, he doesn't know what time of day it is. He came in late on Monday, walked through the factory at ten past eight, there wasn't a machine running and he didn't even notice until I told him. So don't try and tell me he has any clear idea about receiving projection figures. . . .'

He let the words tail away and in the silence which followed and the cold, frosty air of assessment emanating from Brian, he knew he had said too much.

'He's a good man, no denying it, just needs time to develop.' The afterthought sounded just that. Edgar shifted position uneasily; he had cut across Brian's team spirit approach. Brian looked at him as if to say 'Finished?' When he spoke his words were even and cold.

'I am fully aware of the situation here on Monday. Alan gave me a full report, voluntarily. The late start was a reaction to . . .', he searched for the name, '. . . Perryman's death. You, Edgar, do not seem as aware of what is happening in your own area as you are of other people's. The catalogues were not withdrawn on time in five of your territories. I want to know why.'

Edgar's heart jumped as knife blade flashes of panic drew deep slits within him. His jaw had clamped tightly shut but otherwise he had managed to keep control over his expression, outwardly matching Brian's lack of emotion. He got up slowly and went to the filing cabinet. His fingers could have pulled the memo out immediately; he had checked the file so many times but he paused just long enough then returned to his desk, pushing the piece of paper emphatically towards Brian.

He waited as the memo was read. The small gesture of Brian's hand was contemptuous and said, 'So what?'

'A full report, Edgar. Time is short.'

7.18 am

He gazed at the door long after Brian had gone, perfectly still but burning up inside. Sometimes all the undiluted bile from his past life would surface and focus itself on one person or place or event; the acidic substance threatened to burn a way out of him. He consciously unclenched his hands on the desk.

He had to side-step this one, get on with something else and return to it later when things were calmer. Something else, but what? Thoughts closed down the idea. It was always him versus the rest. They all hated his ability to get out ahead. He hated right back their ability to dredge up from deep inside this indigestible knot of feelings best left in the dark where they belonged, where they had lived for years. It gave them a power over him though none of them knew it. Keeping it hidden was his pride.

Edgar felt vaguely annoyed when his right hand reached out automatically to answer the telephone and his lips said 'Broughton' into the mouthpiece without instruction.

'Hello, Alan. An unexpected pleasure at this hour – what appears to be your problem?'

And when the conversation was over and his hand had replaced the receiver – it was his problem. He was lumbered with looking after the visitors. And why not, he thought, and who better to tell him than Henson?

He closed his eyes and rubbed at them wearily. He ought to feel like this at the end of the day not the beginning. But where was his resolve? It was there – somewhere – amongst the angered waves, breaking. It would surface soon. He scanned the mess inside as if trying to sight a survivor. *They* had this power over him; *they* caused all this. If he just sat for a while, calmly, it would subside, everything would be all right.

He picked up the minutes to the last meeting and sat back. If anyone came in they would think he was reading but he sat forward in response to the telephone, again, involuntarily.

'Broughton. Yes, Brian. Mm. OK. Nine o'clock tomorrow and not on Friday. I see. Fine.'

And back went the receiver. The meeting had been brought forward. Why not? He put the minutes back on the desk as if picking them up had caused it. The path of the day was darkening. He would be tied up with the visitors later; there was the meeting to be prepared for and Brian's answers to be arrived at, thought up, if necessary – so, why was he just sitting there?

He just had to wait. This feeling belonged to bedtime where it could be controlled, not at the office; it never came to him here, but his past came down on the flood-tide nevertheless. Flickering images, seen as if under stroboscopic lights. Old movies run at the wrong speed, black and white, backwards through the years, too fast. Running even faster as memories than when they were real and 'now'. Rita was there, frozen into that day when she walked out, unheard of since. Lawrence, twenty years old when she left. Ten years of water twisted round how many bends. Lawrence was at university then – where now? Ten years of water and they, always on the opposite bank but where were the bridges. Where? His son would be thirty now, the same as Henson or Neil, but he was a cuckoo, from nowhere, somehow, so unlike him, certainly not like Rita.

Where now? If Neil had been his son ...

There were footsteps along the corridor. The machine noise took advantage of his attention and made its presence heard. He looked blankly at his desk. ...

8.05 am

More footsteps, stepping on the quiet outside. Carefully, he unstrapped his watch and laid it on the desk, looking at its shifting, melting figures second splitting. Before the digital watch, tenths and hundredths of seconds hardly existed, except on the TV screen at athletics meetings.

He picked up the minutes again yet couldn't read them, but they obscured the minutes on the desk. It was what he wanted to do – pick up the minutes – what he was waiting to do but, obscured or not they ran on without him. He could only sit there in a state of bewilderment, against his will almost. The tide of his thoughts would not recede.

His mind was splitting into two distinct levels; on one, the old movies were running over and over, on the other attempts were still being made to unravel the implications of Brian's words.

The footsteps returned, pausing outside his door. Sally came in

111

with the mail. He let the minutes fall to hide the watch. His eyes followed her as usual, appraising her body out of sheer habit but with as much attention as he had paid the minutes. Her eyes, as usual, avoided his.

He wondered if she had seen the watch. She gave a formal smile as she put the letters on his desk.

'Are those memos ready, Sally? The ones I gave you yesterday.'

It was vital that no one should catch even the faintest hint of his inner disarray.

'Not yet, Mr Broughton. I'll finish them as soon as the post is done. Angela could do them at nine when she comes in. I could ask her if they're urgent.'

She could even talk without actually looking at him.

'No, no. Later will do.'

He watched her leave. He left the letters undisturbed. From nowhere in his mind came the words – a cup of coffee is the answer. Immediately a mental search pattern started up for the question. The word 'memo' was retained also. The old movies were fading, at least this was constructive. Two pieces of a jig-saw. Why weren't the books withdrawn in five of the territories?

If a cup of coffee was the answer, he had better go and get one. He was grateful to be released from the chair, moving again. He caught a glimpse of Sally's bottom as she disappeared into Myers's office. Neil was walking towards him. Edgar smiled warmly; he was owed a favour.

'Neil, the very chap. Morning.'

'Morning, heard about the meeting?'

'Yes, brought forward, tricky that really – look, I need a small favour....' He noted the almost invisible screen of caution fall instantly over Neil's expression. 'Just a small one, a party of visitors, I wondered if...'

'Sorry, Edgar.' Neil shrugged in mock helplessness. 'I'd have been glad to, but I've got to see Brian at eleven. They'll be here at ten-thirty, I believe. Sorry and all that...'

And he was walking off, obviously well clear of the doldrums that had quietened him yesterday.

Edgar continued towards the coffee machine, annoyance and frustration dripping calmly into his anger.

But now there were three pieces to the puzzle as, inexplicably, Neil was retained also. The machine hummed busily as he waited for

112

the cup to fill, clicking when it was finished just as the penny in his mind dropped and he had all the pieces he needed. All he had to do was make them fit. Sally walked by, the basket empty.

8.45 am

Having all the pieces was one thing, making them fit quite another. The coffee stood by the minutes, going cold. He cursed the slowness of his thoughts and the cotton wool blanket that seemed to be holding them back. He rubbed absently at the niggling little pain in his chest. Dimly, the sequence of events which had occurred last week jigged into place. As it dawned on him his hand went up to run his fingers through his hair but it knocked over the coffee. He watched, remotely, as it spread over the minutes.

Last week. The coffee had spilled that day too, only he was at the coffee machine. Sally brought him the withdrawal memo, one original, nine photostats and as he brought the cup out of the machine he had foolishly spilled some over them. Fortunately the original escaped unharmed. He made his mistake then. He signed the original there and sent her off to rephotostat it, leaving her to see to the distribution. Normally he would have done that himself; he trusted no one with anything of importance, but they were so urgent and he was due at a meeting.

Neil had passed him as he took what remained of the coffee down the corridor. He had let him pass then glanced back over his shoulder, to steal a look at Sally's bottom. Neil had caught up with her, teasing her, his arm round her shoulders.

Neil. There was the answer. Neil? So what? Big deal. Yes, quite a big deal for a young man itching for promotion and not wanting to be scratched. He wouldn't be either. Edgar knew he could never prove it. Prove what?

Edgar speculated sadly. It would have to be Neil. Sally had perhaps been a bit upset because he had blamed her for his own clumsiness. Neil, overhearing as he walked towards them, was on hand to sympathize, put his arm round her, perhaps offering to run them off for her?

Bloody fool, just guess-work. The books *were* withdrawn. His former certainty would not be broken down so easily. 'The

catalogues were not withdrawn on time in five of your territories.'
Brian's words poked back at him through the cotton wool. Clever
Neil. Keep five memos back; send out only those for the experienced men who would withdraw anyway. Just what he would have
done. It might take two, maybe three days before Edgar or the
newer salesmen latched on to what was happening. Clever Neil.

He felt very old, very sad as he picked up the minutes. The pool of
coffee escaped on to the watch. He made no attempt to save it. Why
should he? In a lifetime, how much time had he saved? Why not use
it now? Beneath the brown film the liquid crystal numbers still
punched out their urgent message.

It was all guess-work, yes, but absolutely correct, the feeling
between his shoulder blades told him so.

The numbers rearranged themselves to read 9.00. He was startled
as the little alarm on the watch began its cry bravely, then it splut-
tered pathetically as the coffee got to it. He had set the alarm so that
he could gauge how much he had managed to get through before his
official start time at nine. He had solved the reason for his disquiet
but made no progress with his preparations for the meeting. That
didn't seem to matter, now. What did?

Eventually the tiny alarm stopped spluttering and there was
silence. The old movies were showing again. He groaned. Perhaps
he should pick up the telephone, ask Brian for a few days' leave. He
felt quite ill but there was no way out there. Brian would never agree
at this time of year. Anyway, it would be a silent admission of all he
was accused of. Failure, that's what it would be an admission of.

'I've got to see Brian at eleven...' Neil's words echoed back at
him. Promotion, of course. Neon lights in Neil's head not Edgar's. It
had to be Neil – in Brian's shoes who would I have picked, he
thought. Edgar at fifty-two or Edgar at thirty-two? You were never
in it. Long, long past it.

He was the fugitive in all of the old movies playing in his head,
only, the getaway car refused to start and they were closing in. They,
they, *they*! Anger finally escaped him. Bitterness twisted his hands
into fists and he slammed the right one down on to the watch face.
Blood trickled from the heel of his hand but the movies ran on and
back – all the way back to the main feature. They were settling down
to watch. Marion in the restaurant, all those years ago when he was
twenty and so much in love.

But he wouldn't think about *that*, he *wouldn't*. God damn those memories. God damn all of them. It was him versus the rest, just as it had always been and he would run out the winner like he always had. Devil take the hindmost but it wouldn't be him.

Sometimes, against all the odds, the car starts and then there is the chase scene....

9.45 am

'Bette? Are you leaving?' She asked the question and immediately wished she had given it more thought. Bette frowned but continued working.

'If I am, I'm the last to hear of it but then, that's usually the way with rumours.'

'Sorry, I...'

'Oh, that's ok, Sally.' She stopped checking the report and sat back. 'Rumours are fun, aren't they? Especially if you're not involved. I enjoy speculating on the turn of events myself but I tend to keep my own council and use my eyes – not just my ears.'

Sally continued with the filing. She smiled but didn't really see what Bette meant.

'Sally, I've been meaning to have a chat. It doesn't look as if Angela will be coming in today. There's a chance we might not be interrupted so, come and sit down.'

She felt a little knot of nerves in her stomach as she sat opposite Bette, wondering what was coming.

'Sometimes, by using your eyes you can spot tomorrow's rumour, not just listen to today's.' Bette's tone was firm but sympathetic.

'I'm not sure what you mean.'

'I'd guess that tomorrow's rumour is going to be you and Alan....'

'But there's nothing...' Sally was annoyed and could feel herself blushing.

'ok, ok. And I'm not leaving, either. See? There doesn't have to be any truth in it, does there?'

Sally remained silent, not quite sure what line to take, uncertain whether she wanted the conversation to develop or not and yet wanting desperately to talk to someone. The Alan–Gary thing had churned itself into a messy tangle.

115

'I know I'm sticking my neck out, Sally, but I'd like to help. You probably think I don't understand but, if you'll allow, let's see what using your eyes and a bit of restrained guess-work can do. May I?'

Sally nodded but remained defensive.

'Stop me when I go wrong. You were in a bit of a state on Monday. At first I thought it was Jim's death alone but then sensed there was something else as well. Alan was in a bit of a state too, has been for some time. Jim's death came on top of that. But it doesn't matter what the causes were – we have two people floundering and realizing that nothing stops: nothing rests just because they're feeling rotten: the world just goes right on over them and they'll go under – or will they?'

She nodded again, wanting her to continue. Bette was surprisingly sympathetic and seemed to be taking great care not to upset her.

'So – one notices the other's distress, swims over and lends a hand. Alan keeping your head above water, I'd guess, and giving you just enough strength to keep from going under. And you're grateful – right?'

'Mm.'

'And now you're in love?'

'How did you...?'

'I've seen how you react whenever he comes into the office; it wasn't there last week, this week it is.'

'Yes, but it's not that easy...'

'No, I know – there's the young man who phoned you here last night. From what little I heard of his voice, I'd say he might be in a bit of a state too. Yes?'

Bette's accuracy made her feel uncomfortable – transparent and shallow. She was about to react to it when Bette said, 'I'm not questioning the fact that you're in love with Alan. Alan probably loves you.' The words came as a shock to her.

'Then – why is it so wrong. I mean...?'

'Yes, it does feel wrong, doesn't it? One of the things you learn as you go along – loving and being in love – they're not the same.'

'But you said Alan loves me.'

'Yes, I loved Jim Perryman and I know you did. I'm fairly sure Alan did. There's being in love and then there are several different kinds of loving. Simple,' she said, smiling suddenly. 'All you need to

116

do is find someone you're in love with, who's in love with you and who loves you in as many different ways as possible. Easy! And all in one person. Easy.' There was a tinge of bitterness in her voice and her smile faded momentarily.

Sally laughed and the tension was released.

'But do you really think it's Alan?'

Her smile faded a little and the confusion was still there. Despite this she could see what Bette was driving at.

'I think you're right but – oh it all seems so easy when you say it; when I think it out alone it all gets tangled up again.'

'Yes, it has a habit of doing that, I'm afraid. I know I'm an interfering old dragon but I think you probably love Alan as a friend – as he loves you. The guess-work gets less restrained as I go on but I'd say you may have helped Alan to stay afloat too. You were there, needing him, and helping you took him away from his own problems, even if only for a short while. Can't go under if someone else needs you just at that moment, can you? Maybe the boy on the phone needs someone, like you did.'

'Gary? Perhaps. I don't know – we've had problems. He wants to talk. I think I can understand what you mean.'

'Men and women – they can be *friends* you know, not just targets for one another with a double bed as the bull's eye.'

She laughed. Neil put his head round the door, noted Angela's empty desk and seemed relieved.

'Leave these with you, Bette, not too urgent, see you.'

Bette smiled as the door closed.

'Mind you, that last remark isn't a hard and fast rule, you understand?'

They both laughed. Sally got up and returned to the filing cabinet.

'I'm glad you're not leaving,' she said happily, 'and thanks – you interfere beautifully.'

The telephone rang. Bette answered it, smiling.

9.55 am

Edgar sat at Brian's desk, lounged might have been a better word. Brian continued to check over a sheet of figures using the old, make 'em wait and sweat tactic. Edgar looked around the room,

117

unconcerned, now in complete control and proud of it. At last Brian looked up. With a satisfied sigh he tidied away the papers.

'Sorry, Edgar, had to get those cleared.'

Edgar shrugged.

'No matter. These visitors – how many and what's been laid on?'

'A dozen – you saw the list, didn't you? They're middle managers from the new firm – some already are, some are hoping to be. Usual drill – show them round the factory – let the department heads explain their methods. Out to lunch. Bette has got all that booked, usual place. Bring them back here; give them the film show on company history – that's laid on in the Conference Room. Then you can hand them over to us. Bette is going to give them a little talk. I'll try and inject a bit of team spirit into them and that's it. All *very* routine, Edgar.' He sounded bored.

Edgar raised an eyebrow at the use of the word 'us' and at Bette's role, that wasn't routine. He noted with satisfaction that Brian seemed to take the gesture as comment on the slight sarcasm.

'Right, I see. Now – this so-called crisis, how are we doing with it?'

Edgar was pleased with the way things were going, aggression was the only way to back Brian off, wrest the initiative and leave him to wonder which of the two was Managing Director.

'We're pulling through, thanks to Alan. Despatch are coping admirably. I'm very pleased with David's response. They're on two shifts from today. We're on a knife-edge still but another night shift like last night and we might have bought enough time to salvage the situation....'

Edgar cut in quickly, knowing that after his praise for Alan and David he would break back with a sarcastic shot for him.

'Good – glad to hear it. You were quite right this morning – five of my salesmen hadn't withdrawn the books despite my instructions. I have issued fairly mild reprimands to those concerned; that's all I feel it warrants. That's it, Brian. I want it dropped.'

Now Brian's eyebrows were raised.

'Now, look, Edgar – let's get this clear...'

'It's perfectly clear, Brian. It's been a hard year. A large proportion of my team is new but they're damned good and I'm not having a major issue made out of what is merely their enthusiasm. The fat is out of the fire and no harm done. It's a good team I'm building and I don't want it spoiled.'

118

If only he had taken this tack when he saw Brian earlier. Brian waved his hand, acceding.

'All right, leave it there. With regard to the amount of harm done, we'll let the accountants put a figure on that later. Some of it could be finding its way into your budget, or, rather, out of it. We'll see if you're willing to minimize it then. Now all you have to do is explain away why I didn't get a copy of the projection, nor David Myers and – more important, Alan Henson, until Monday. . . .'

'Henson had the figures on *Thursday*!', Edgar snapped. 'They were so urgent I foolishly agreed to let him see to copies and distribution.'

Hold firm on this, thought Edgar, glaring across at him. Just how much time is he prepared to spend on running a lie to ground? He wouldn't dare get rid of me anyway, too useful. Promote Telford if you must. I can pull his strings and he won't even know. The two men continued to glare at each other and Edgar waited to see which way he would jump.

'Edgar.' He was having difficulty holding down his temper. Edgar watched implacably as a scarlet flush rose up his neck. 'You're good, no one denies it but you either work with the team or you find yourself leafing through the company pension book – to see how much you're due. Any more politics, any more cock-ups and I warn you . . .'

Edgar remained impassive, watching him trying to find words and a way of keeping the lid on his temper.

He calmed down. 'I'd also like to make it quite clear that none of this brought any influence to bear on the decision I intend to announce at tomorrow's meeting. So just think yourself lucky.'

The audience was at an end and in the half an hour or so before he was due to welcome the visitors, Edgar found himself turning those final words over and over in his mind. The eternal optimist, he wasn't *quite* ready to give up yet. Think yourself lucky, I've promoted you despite the last few days or, think yourself lucky you've still got a job, never mind promotion. Optimism and pessimism alternated – but there was still a flicker of hope.

10.30 am

It was a long time before he actually saw the faces of the visitors. They met in reception. He took them up to the Conference Room. Brian was there with a welcome – and Bette. Edgar was too busy pondering on this fact and watching Brian give his performance to notice much about them as people. There were a couple of women and the usual sprinkling of keen eyed, self assured young men, some faceless plodders – a standard bunch.

He was sitting at the conference table viewing the deadly boring prospect of showing them around, answering their usual and never varying visitors' questions, when it all changed: it all suddenly changed.

The attentive profile of one of the women caught his eye. It was her copper coloured hair and her profile and it was Marion. His heart rate doubled. Everything stopped. He looked away, looked again. It was Marion and it wasn't and it *was*.

Edgar swallowed hard and looked away from her, excitement and fear in his stomach, acceptance and disbelief in his mind. There was a pounding throb in his chest; his throat was dry, his eyes fixed.

A full scale alert in his mind tried to stabilize the effects from the violent alternations going through him. He couldn't keep his eyes from her for long – she was sitting there, after all those years, all those years of unhappiness. He had to look. Something long dead was stirring inside, forcing a way up through all the cold and concrete thoughts he had poured over any of the memories or ideals attached to her. The concrete had been tipped over the ill-prepared foundations which were all he had to rebuild on after she hurt him so badly. Cracks spreading, darkness falling into them, deep, black and going down.

She turned her head, looked him full in the face and she kept on looking but without a trace of recognition. He became horrifyingly aware that everyone else in the room was looking too.

'Edgar?' Brian's voice crashed through to him.

'What? Sorry, I was ...'

'I was just explaining about today's programme ...'

'Yes, – yes, of course. I will be introducing you to each head of department in turn and I'd like you to be completely unrestrained with your questions....'

120

And it was like throwing a switch on a cassette. The tape played over as it had so many times before and he struggled to keep his eyes from her.

Inside – there was the renewed bedlam of the stroboscopic lights and the main feature was beginning all over again, flickering out the scene with her in the restaurant. This time she was wearing the dark blue, woollen dress she had on now and not looking in the least out of place even though the other couple with whom they had shared that evening were dressed in the fashion of the period.

'. . . now, this is all very formal. I suggest that we go down to the dining-room where coffee will be served and I can talk to you individually.'

The tape came to an end and he was back in the room and they were getting up.

He caught a glimpse of her as she went out and, in the corner of his eye, the searching glance Bette gave him as she held open the door. He followed.

The eye of the hurricane – that's what the last two hours were, he thought as they moved down the corridor. The period of time when the eye passes directly overhead and all is calm – until it moves on and the storm follows. There were no getaway cars available and no sign of the cavalry coming over the hill top.

10.39 am

They were all standing around in the dining-room drinking coffee, talking shop. Brian was with her, laughing. Livid green strands of jealousy shot through him.

'Yes, indeed,' he heard himself saying to the aggressive young man he was with. 'That is a very real danger. It's so easy for a company, or any corporate body, to grow beyond its optimum size. However, if the dangers are recognized the problem is controllable – I would have thought.'

I would have thought, said a nonsense voice inside him. I would have thought but I couldn't, so I didn't – but I would have thought that thought ought to be controllable – wouldn't you think?

He moved away from the young man, sweating slightly. He

121

introduced himself to another who might well have been the same person for all the difference there appeared to be.

The feeling between his shoulder blades came back and he realized it had never really gone away. In his mind's eye he was scanning down the list of visitors' names.

'. . . yes, it's liable to change at any time, of course, and this market is particularly fickle. You have to find the trend, run it down and stay with it; change when it does. If you're strong enough you can actually set the trend, hopefully.'

No hope. Should have heeded the warning. That feeling between your shoulders – not Neil and the projection, not Brian but the name on the list you tried to skimp over without seeing. M. Ansell. Marion. All the way down beneath the concrete.

'. . . concrete figures are difficult to come by. We produced all our Christmas stock during the summer, despatched it to retail shops in the autumn. What you will see us working on later are what we call private orders, dealing with customers direct. People who want their names and addresses printed inside. It's a continuous process. Our next Christmas range is already completed. We're busy all year. It never stops . . .'

Time does, watches run down, can't stop them. But a watch is not time, it's times – a multiplier. Positive, negative. Time is a divider and equals only your own speed. . . .

When she was standing in front of him there was quiet, stillness and the violent shift out of bedlam was as frightening as the madhouse. Even in the still calm there was no peace. This moment stepping out of line, frozen. All those images of her blurring out of all the shadows in his mind. Her face – she hadn't changed at all.

'I hope you will enjoy your visit here, Miss . . .?' He seemed to be saying, though it didn't sound like him but when she answered she was using someone else's voice too.

'Ansell. It's very impressive, so far. I'm particularly looking forward to seeing your Production Control department. I've heard a lot about it.'

Her lips were the same, her teeth, the shade and texture of her hair. Green-blue eyes faintly smiling when she spoke but not even a vague hint of recognition in them and it wasn't Marion's voice.

So the question marks came, falling in diagonal lines, raining down on his certainty, washing it away and setting up a new one – just as certain: this wasn't Marion.

Edgar felt it go all through him, emotions spiralling, swirling – water down a drain. He was fighting hard now just to stay where he was, not follow it down. In its wake, something like exhaustion and all the churned up mud left to dry.

He broke away from her as quickly as he could, falling into another set of words. Someone else talking and the tape machine playing out the answers in the talking game. But he had to keep glancing across at her – when she was instantly Marion and then not at all.

She hadn't changed. All those years with a watch on his wrist, running through it, marking it out. Then, when he meets her again he overlooks the most obvious thing of all – that it can't be her because time moves on and, to be her, she would have to look older thirty-odd years later. Time strapped on to your wrist and you still ignore its passing. This must be her daughter.

'... time factors playing a crucial role, of course. We use the facilities of our parent company pretty extensively – hiring time from their computer. Time-sharing has made a big difference ...'

Minute to minute he was making it. What else could he do? Crack up completely? If he walked outside, jibbering out loud all the nonsense that was twitching its way through his head, he wouldn't get as far as the car-park before wishing he was back here. Wondering what was going on. Far better to stand here, he thought, wondering what's going on.

11.01 am

Sensors told him that the time to begin the tour had settled over the gathering. More tapes played and he took the party down to the shop floor. The noise drilled at him, twisting in and out of his explanations of what was going on but, from inside, greater noise roared back at the factory, excluding it.

As his mother and father were nag, nag, nagging at him to do well at school and get ahead he was parrying a question from one of the young men. His hands moved quickly and his voice pulled up out of the noise as he explained the processes, the bright colours moving swiftly along. His parents were coming at him with renewed pressure – once out ahead he'd got to stay there. Staying ahead was

123

the measure marked out on the wall which they pushed him up against.

More questions, left and right, one from Marion but – what was her real name? He answered her in some depth, moving closer to her, protected by the noise. Inside, the strobe lights beat slowly between her being Marion and not being – but at least the tempo was slower.

He walked alongside her down the centre aisle of the factory, the others followed. Let the others follow, said his parents. Let the others live, another voice had said. That other voice, so quiet and gentle with such hard things to say as it railed and rebelled against the straight and narrow jacket they were pushing him into.

His arm ached to slip round her shoulders as they moved on, stopping at the next section and regrouping around him. Another tape unwound and she listened to it intently as he listened to the music now going through his head, Glen Miller's *In the Mood* as it had been playing all those years ago in the restaurant.

On that night, the quieter of the two voices had been defeated. It had become a matter of the survival of the loudest and there was no contest. Victory got out ahead and he had to follow and he had to stay there – out in front and running from the ashes of that evening's defeat.

Edgar moved them into Stores and Despatch. It was quieter, the noise more spaced out and discernible. Fork lift trucks racked up pallets of work into a bulk storage area and people moved along the aisles of smaller racks, making up orders. There was the sound of a lorry reversing up to the loading bay and the factory drummed in the distance.

He filtered out the questions. When everything had been explained he took them slowly back through the noise and the machines and the tired faces. Up above, behind the glass, he caught sight of Henson moving swiftly along the corridor. Neil was coming out of Brian's office. Henson paused to speak. Sally passed them as Bette disappeared into Myers's office.

11.50 am

He took them back to the Conference Room, an immense feeling of calm within him and one of inevitability. Minute by minute he had clawed his way through the morning. Even a hurricane has to blow itself out. He didn't trust this feeling; it was almost as difficult to deal with as the emotional mangling he had survived – but he had survived. Minute by minute, stacked one on top of another. For most of the morning he had been operating on several levels simultaneously, all under attack. He had coped.

A general discussion was developing, easily and naturally.

'It's all too easy,' he was saying, 'to fall into the trap. If you think of yourselves purely as problem solvers it becomes too easy to see only the short term considerations. Respond to them, yes – there will always be crises, but you can find yourself just lurching from one to another. In the long term ...'

Long term, middle term. Forwards and backwards. There is always now, seemingly constant but always moving.

Edgar moved on, taking them around the departments, watching them all. Henson was first. He spoke briefly, obviously wanting to be free of them as quickly as possible. He answered their questions well. There were several from Marion. Ironic, he thought, that she should concern herself with Production.

In his view, the gulf between Production and Sales remained as wide as ever despite Brian's 'team spirit'. The music came back to him as he watched Henson's lips move. He noted the shadows round his eyes and the strain in his voice, the stress in his hands. His own fingers were tapping out *In the Mood*. He listened to the stranger's voice coming from Marion's lips and outside there was the sound of the machines – running.

They moved on to Neil's office. A different man. Edgar watched. Henson's words had been spare and ill-prepared, either separating out with long pauses in between or sticking to one another, getting themselves in the wrong order. Neil's words coasted, unfaltering, ideas as passengers. Edgar watched closely whenever his eyes rested on Marion as they frequently did. He watched her too but could detect no response to Neil's obvious interest. She asked no questions.

He could see her lack of interest now – why not all those years ago? Marion had always despised him – because of his background?

125

Perhaps she had even hated him. She was very cut glass. It must have been a kind of hatred.

Neil would be joining them for lunch. Edgar smiled on the outside, laughed hysterically inside. Oh, leave her alone, you fool, he wanted to say. Can't you see she doesn't even *like* you ... but then, Neil might soon be Managing Director, he had been just a trainee salesman.

He listened to Myers which was more than anyone else seemed to be doing – there isn't much glamour in Stores and Despatch. But there was a change in him, he spoke with less reserve than usual. There was a new enthusiasm in his eyes. Perhaps he had been offered the post.

The pendulum still stroked its way from side to side and, during the times when he thought it wasn't going to be him, Edgar realized that he would have to swallow it, survive and start to get ahead all over again. It was nearly lunchtime.

1.00 pm

The business talk filled the restaurant; Edgar was only partially aware of it. He sat next to Neil and opposite Marion. Alienated from the scene around him, he watched and played tapes out across the table, nothing seemed capable of affecting him now. Nothing could touch him. He watched her smiling across at Neil, politely. He was playing tapes of his own, prerecorded at how many different restaurants? How many pairs of eyes had laughed at these words? Edgar could only hear the strains of *In the Mood*. He watched her hands and her eyes.

A shadowy restaurant in 1946, sparse and under-populated. It had an excellent reputation and was known to offer a reasonable menu – if you had the money. The strobe lights had stopped flickering now and the scene was clear. It had been playing over all these years but he had never allowed himself to watch. He looked on now with contempt, as he sensed the waiter had. He saw himself as he was then through the waiter's eyes.

The young man with Marion. His eyes were full of ideals and dreams and Marion. But she was there without justification, the

126

waiter could see that, he amused her. This was their first evening together, one shared by Charles and Lucy.

He was a poet then, so he thought, rebelling against his parents, so it seemed. A young man in a restaurant he couldn't really afford with people not of his class. Marion's father might own the place for all he knew – or the ground it stood on.

His parents were newly arrived in the middle classes with hardly anything unpacked except their bigotry and their snobbery, ferociously set out on display. His poetry took a mutinous stand against their values – yet here he was, striving to push aside his class just as fiercely as they and there wasn't much of the poet at the table that evening.

The waiter brought the wine.

'I'm trying to convince Madeline of the folly of her ways, Edgar.' Neil came into focus. 'She's Production orientated, I'm afraid.'

'Madeline?'

'Madeline Ansell,' she said, smiling.

'I knew your mother, Marion.' She showed no surprise.

'Really?' she said dismissively. 'My father's a shareholder, you know, of your parent company.'

He didn't know. He didn't want to know. As they looked across at one another coolly, he sensed that Neil was hanging on every word.

'You were asking some very searching questions of our Mr Henson, this morning,' he said, looking away from her.

'Yes, he's excellent, isn't he? You're very lucky ...'

Neil interrupted then, launching another good-natured attack on the Production Departments of the world and Edgar faded back into the shadows.

It was Marion and Edgar, Charles and Lucy. Even his cynicism and the years could not dull the elation when she asked him to make up the foursome, the clear indication that he would be with her. A mad panic had followed searching for a restaurant which offered something outside the fixed price menu. Food and money were scarce. It had surprised him – then – the lengths he had been prepared to go to, scraping enough together.

He watched her as she spoke to Neil, in her eyes a cool and steady dislike veiled by polite responses and sexual come-ons. He doubted if Neil saw it. Come on, they seemed to say, get on to the hook, it won't hurt, promise it won't hurt.

She had led him on, played teasing games. Suggestions were made so that he would misunderstand – he did and she kept the line slack enough to ensure his continued interest. She brought him out of the swimmy idealistic waters all the way up to the dinner-table.

The evening was a great success until he reached across the table and covered her hand with his. She brushed it aside, making some remarks everyone laughed at – he joined in. There was a lot of laughter that evening but things kept clicking and checking inside because he couldn't avoid the feeling that, binding all the separate parcels of laughter together, there was one big joke he wasn't in on. He tried to brush it aside, much as she had done with his hand. But he was a great success, though sometimes it seemed as if they were laughing only at his voice and not at his words. He looked forward to taking her home, being alone with her, perhaps even kissing her. In the endless, expectant days leading up to their date that was all he had looked forward to.

'Now listen, darling,' she said, finally, 'you're really very sweet and you're not to get upset or disappointed but we've got a surprise which I *know* you'll be thrilled about. . . .'

And while she was bubbling all this over him, Charles was taking a small box from his pocket. He watched, disbelief freezing him as the engagement ring slipped on to her finger. They all seemed pent up and eager to laugh but held back from it.

'You're the very first to know, darling – well, nearly.'

'But . . . Charles and Lucy . . . I thought . . .'

'Lucy's his *sister*, silly boy, surely you knew that? Oh, Charles and I are *so* happy and Daddy has invited literally thousands of people and they're all waiting at this moment! None of them *know*, well, most of them don't. Thanks awfully for the bite . . .'

And through all this they were standing up and Charles was getting the coats from the waiter.

'We simply *must* dash, Daddy will be waiting to announce it; isn't it *wonderful*. It'll be in *The Times* tomorrow. . . .'

He remained seated, stupefied. The entire evening dismantled in minutes and all the days before and all the tomorrows he'd dreamed of – wiped. As they left their laughter escaped. It went out with them and found a way, all the way, back to him as they faded down the street.

'Thanks awfully for the bite . . .' Her words refused to drown in the last of the wine he stayed to drink. The waiter seemed to be eyeing him suspiciously as he went about his task as if he knew Edgar might not have enough to cover the bill.

Edgar tried to remember all they had ordered and cost it. In a state of growing panic he couldn't get the numbers to add up. It would be the final humiliation if he couldn't pay. He caught the waiter's eye, swallowing hard as he approached.

'Sir?'

'Could I have the bill, please?'

The man smiled, a hint of contempt in his eyes.

'Mr Ansell attended to that, sir,' he said in a polished accent.

Edgar couldn't mask his relief. Flamboyantly he stood up, pressing some money in the waiter's hand but he caught him by the elbow, discreetly pulling him back as he tried to pass.

'Don't be silly, son,' he said quietly in a different voice. 'You can't afford it, can you?'

He could see the unspoken words in his eyes, 'know your place'.

'I'm sorry if I creased your hire suit, sir.' His voice had regained its polish. 'Good evening.'

Edgar walked home, the lights of the big house on the hill burning in his eye corner.

He found himself in the restaurant again and they were all getting up to leave. It was like coming out from a matinée performance at the cinema. When the film is over, it's difficult to believe that it's daylight outside.

Since that evening he had never tipped another waiter. He looked on as Neil left some money in a saucer.

He automatically glanced at his watch as they prepared to leave, forgetting he had taken it off. He had no idea what time it was.

2.35 pm

Shadows. From the restaurant, from the darkness of that long walk home – they collected now in the Conference Room, darkened for the film show.

He watched the screen and the company history unfolded for the four-thousandth time. The clicking of the projector rhythmed its way into him, matching the beat of the stroboscopic lights which had now returned once more.

129

She was sitting next to him at the back, Marion, Madeline, whatever her name was. He hadn't engineered it that way, maybe she had wanted to escape Neil. He was still with them, more attentive towards her than ever. Probably the mention of 'Daddy's shares', he thought.

In the backlash days which followed that night, he discovered that it is never possible for anyone to be as cruel to you as you are to yourself. Mercilessly he fed it all through, mauling the exposed nerve until it became numb. He waited for it all to subside and then manhandled any thoughts of her out of the way. There was just the débris left and amongst it he found ambition and determination and he found the Game.

Without turning his head, he looked at her from the corner of his eye. Her legs were crossed. Pity, he thought.

The game had evolved from his sense of rejection and failure. It meant avoiding hooks and using the rules of society, its hidden prejudices, to good advantage. If what he had wanted to give wasn't good enough then the answer was simple – TAKE. It was their fault, not his.

She uncrossed her legs and watched the film, seeming slightly less bored than everyone else. He could reach out and put his hand on her thigh, slide it upwards between her legs. What could she say? He would only accuse her of encouraging him if she dared to make a fuss. The men in the room would take his part and condemn her – each making a mental note that this one was 'a bit of a lass', Edgar a 'bit of a lad'.

The women wouldn't take his part but they wouldn't take hers either because she had 'made a fuss' and they had probably experienced something similar and either been forced to keep quiet or found some other way of dealing with it. All of which would be too late.

Edgar's hand remained where it was. He had never taken from Marion and, besides, there was too much danger here. The game was best played in husband and wife situations, less risk there. The wife dare not protest – the husband would always wonder if she *had* encouraged him and all the other men in the room would *know* she had.

He didn't do it for sexual pleasure, that – if it came – was a bonus. The real excitement came from *taking* – without permission, without violence and within the laws of the social circle. The vicious circle, as he saw it. This appealed to the aching, festering nerve within him. And it was dangerous and fun.

His hand slipped inside his jacket and rubbed at his chest. He scanned over the events of the morning. He *still* loved her. That was all that came clearly out of the thirty-two years that stood between them. It startled him – it seemed that love could not be destroyed only heated up further and warped. All that concrete he had poured over it left more débris now than there had ever been.

In the space of a few hours the dreamer he had been, or tried to be, and the man he had become were thrown into stark relief under the stroboscopic light. Each momentary view of himself being greeted with derision and contempt, loathing from each side within.

He raised his hand, closed his eyes and rubbed at them, as if he could squeeze out the tiredness and the tears. It was a dirty game. Now he knew it. Rita, his wife, discovered it. He had tried to explain but she just said he was dirty. It was the first and last time he had tried to let Marion out of him.

He could see the look on Rita's face just before she walked out – not so different from the way he felt about himself now. The two were in fact an exact match.

He took his hand from his eyes, became aware that the projector was whirring madly and, silhouetted against the blank screen, heads were turned to see what was wrong.

He leapt up and stopped the machine, turned on the lights. He blundered through a mass of words. The tapes were twisted and he couldn't marshall the sounds coming from his mouth into a fluent pattern.

They were all looking at him, fascinated – embarrassed for him and with him.

Bette arrived at his side. He could only feel the pride at getting through the morning gush and rillow its way down and through and out of him.

3.05 pm

He sat at Brian's desk. Brian was with the visitors now. Bette returned looking worried.

'All under control,' she said, attempting a smile. 'I think you ought to see a doctor, Edgar. I'll make arrangements for someone to drive you home.' She went to pick up the phone.

'No,' he said, very quietly. His hand rested on hers briefly and guided the receiver back on its rest; he squeezed it gently. Now he attempted a smile. 'I'll go to the surgery this evening. I can drive myself.' On and on and on, he said under his breath.

'Are you sure?'

'Yes. Don't know what came over me. I'll go home now.'

But he did know. As he made his way to the car, all he could see was Madeline's face and he had started to cry. All he could see was the sympathy in her eyes – it was what he had wanted to see every single day since the scene in the restaurant. It was too much and it was what he couldn't take. The game was over.

He sat in the car a long time then he drove slowly home, deep in winter, darkness already tumbling out of grey, unbroken clouds. There was no explanation for his sister when he arrived home unexpectedly. There were no thoughts in his head. In the semi-dark of his bedroom there was only a crumpled suit on the floor as he pulled the clothes up over him.

Wednesday Night

11.55 pm

Sally hugged herself beneath the bed-clothes, not wanting to let the feeling go – even for sleep.

In Gary's eyes, in his words and the movement of his hands, there was something missing, something she had never noticed when it was there – bravado. His words seemed to be struggling to explain it. His words were awkward, scattered but she *knew*. 'I want to see you again,' he said. He had been out with a couple of girls since their last date but he wanted to be with her.

'Look, this sex thing, I mean, let's just leave it, OK? When we're both ready it'll just happen. I tried to force the pace but it needn't cause any more trouble between us ... only, *please* don't let any of my mates know. They all think ... oh, never mind that, let 'em just think.'

She held him, whispering, 'Oh you silly boy, you silly boy.' And for the first time in her life she felt grown up and clear of the sticky, clinging teenage years.

She hugged herself but relaxed slowly as sleep laid down across all her thoughts, softening the images and fluffing out the edges.

'Edgar went home early today, taken ill or something.'

Caroline nodded and continued to undress. The bedroom was warm. She felt sleepy and relaxed. In the last two days they had stopped fuelling each other's tension.

'All sorts of rumours about it. Neil is going around saying he cracked up, all at once. Can't imagine that somehow.'

'Might have been you, can you imagine that?'

'Oh yes.' He sighed. 'Can't say I feel much sympathy though – if he has gone over. He spends a lot of his time trying to push other people to the edge.'

She combed her hair.

'I've never liked him much but he's very sad, really.'

133

Two years ago, at a dinner party, he had groped her in the kitchen having gallantly insisted that he help her with the coffee. In the split second horror of the moment she hadn't known what to do. Instinct told her she couldn't cry out. All the women knew about him. So this was what they had meant, though when they had related their experiences she had always thought *she* would protest at the top of her voice.

His action had been unprompted, completely without warning or encouragement. She remembered the look in his eyes, cold and calm as his left hand went behind her, squeezing her buttocks and pulling her on to his right hand which forced her evening skirt between her legs and then began to squeeze.

She had stared right back and poured the scalding coffee down him. The ensuing fuss as she apologized profusely was well within the rules and some of the women hid their smiles when they came to see what was wrong.

'Very sad.' She slid into bed and rested her head on David's chest.

'I suppose it's down to Neil and Alan now – promotion.'

'Are you sure it won't be you? Sure it's not what you want?'

'Certain, on both counts.' He cuddled her. 'The others can lie awake tonight, looking for the answers on the ceiling. Let's get some sleep.'

The light went out with a click.

'Yes,' she said, dreamily.

'*No!*' The severity of her voice made him jump, his hand fell away from her breast. 'Don't use sex, Alan, to get yourself out of a corner. Listen to me!'

She took his hand and pulled him over to the dressing-table. 'Sit down and *look*.'

He flopped down on the stool.

'Don't you ever use that thing? The mirror?'

He raised his head, so did the man in the mirror. Nancy stood behind him, anger and love in her eyes.

'How old would you say the fella in there is? Forty-six? Forty-eight? I ordered a wreath for Jim today – want me to increase the order? We might get a discount. See that man in there? He's just got home. He left for work seventeen hours ago: hasn't eaten his supper and in ten minutes will be dead to the world, until the next round. . . .'

134

She began to massage his shoulders and neck, at first vigorously, then more gently.

'And he's been living like this for months.'

He opened his mouth to protest.

'Oh the sixteen hour day is a new and clever innovation – *he thinks*.' She jabbed a finger at the man in the mirror, checking his protest. 'Looks very clever, doesn't he? With the bags under his eyes beginning to show and the red rings under those. Real intellectual.'

'It's almost over, love, nearly there, just tomorrow and Friday, that's all.'

'Alan, it *is* over.' She pushed him in the back to emphasize her words, walking away from him. Suddenly she picked up the digital alarm and yanked its lead from the wall. She hurled it across the room at the door. It smashed, the plastic breaking apart.

'If tomorrow is so bloody important, you'll wake up in time. You can get yourself up.'

Neil waited on the bitterly cold station for the last train of the night back into the city. His car was waiting there. He had travelled with the visitors, had eventually taken Madeline out to dinner. He was flying.

He looked back over the week. Jenny and Judi and Angela, now Madeline but she was different. No games here or perhaps a new one emerging. He had sensed that she expected him to act in a certain way, didn't particularly seem to want it but expected it. The evening had been a catalogue of things he hadn't done. He hadn't tried to seduce her, or touch her. He didn't keep the normal tally on how much drink she had nor try to increase it. Judi would have approved. With Madeline he could fly. Tomorrow he would be Managing Director and on his way upwards. With Madeline – and her father's connections at head office – he could consolidate and lengthen the inroads he had been making into the parent company.

At various points during the evening, he found himself comparing her with Jenny, favourably but he wouldn't let his thoughts of Jenny develop. He was flying. Get lost, he had said.

He drew his coat tighter round him.

The doors slammed and the people moved along the platform heading for the way out. They passed him in a continuous stream, then it broke.

135

'Edgar?'

He was surprised to look up and see Neil standing there.

'Are you OK? Heard you were taken ill or something.'

'Hello, Neil. No, I'm fine. Went home got some sleep. Can't sleep now. Feel great now.' He wished he could make his voice sound more convincing. 'I suppose I was ill, really. Tiredness is an illness if you don't take enough sleep for it.'

'There aren't any more trains tonight. Can I give you a lift?'

'Lift? Good idea, so cold, more snow tonight. Only meant to take a little stroll, think things out.'

They wandered into the car-park. Neil waited patiently as Edgar impatiently tried to remaster the art of getting into a sports car.

'Used to drive a sports job myself,' he said as Neil slammed the door. 'Never think it. Sunbeam Talbot, white walled tyres and wire wheels. Feel old, saying that. Feel so old now anyway.'

'Are you sure you're all right, Edgar. You look ghastly.'

'Fine. I've just been doing some thinking, stayed out too long that's all. Thinking myself round in circles. Haven't done that for years. Chased thoughts, yes, but never allowed them to just happen any old how. You've been chasing Marion, have you?'

'Marion? Oh you mean Madeline. Yes, took her out to dinner.'

'On a winner there, keep at it. Seeing her again?'

'Yes, hope to.'

Edgar thought he didn't sound very sure. He probably never would be with that one. It would do him good.

When he saw the scene in the restaurant clearly, without the strobe lights, he had realized it was a joke, just a joke. She hadn't really meant to hurt him. she hadn't considered his feelings at all. He had walked round the streets thinking about it. Why couldn't he see it then? It didn't matter now but he couldn't help wondering what she really looked like now and whether or not it was still funny.

He saw the sympathy again in Madeline's eyes, heard her mother's laughter.

'On a winner there,' he repeated absently, 'if you throw away the script.'

Neil looked at him quizzically but the rest of the journey passed in silence down the yellow-orange dual carriageway.

. . . . .

136

The wind swooped low into the city, in amongst the glittering towers and the on-off neon strips. It moved down the back alleys, shifting crumpled, screwed up sheets of yesterday's news – moving them on. It slipped out into the suburbs which were sleeping out the darkness or not sleeping in random, scattered squares of yellow. It rattled at the windows, saw who was awake to hear.

The scene ran again. Another forest. Trees all tangled and grown over with shadows seeping from between them like paint spilt over the yellow flatness of the plain.

The Northern riders have gone through: they are now just ahead of the dust haze they are creating, in the shimmering distance. And the Runner is coming. . . .

Hunted he ran, through the trees, out across the plain. He stumbled as he crossed the stream, got up and ran as the riders from the South broke free of the forest. He ran. His ears filled up with the drumming of the horses behind him; his eyes tried to peer through the dust haze of those ahead.

He became aware of the rider pacing him out to the West and the other one in the East on a big, black, nervous horse. He ran faster keeping ahead of those behind him but only just ahead of exhaustion.

Then there was the hill; it hadn't been there before but now it was, threatening his speed. He tried to avoid it but the big horse rode in hard from the East. He zig-zagged. The horseman's speed sent him past and a little ahead but he turned quickly and ran straight at him, avoiding collision only at the last moment.

The Runner veered, found himself back in the path of the hill. He zig-zagged again but the horseman reared up his mountainous horse at him. He ran, his breath rasping now in a chain saw rhythm. Stumbling, he lay momentarily in the fine dust but the drumming racked into him like an electric charge and spasmed him back to his feet.

And he ran and the hill was still ahead and the horseman cut him off, to the left, to the right, putting him in the way of it.

He ran at the slope, desperate and frantic. He tried to take it in his stride without losing speed, pumping more and more energy into his legs. But there was no more. His reserves took him to the top then his legs buckled and he collapsed there. Across the emptiness of the plain there was no sound and no sign of any horsemen.

Sally Warren
Thursday

8.30 am

Sally walked along, swinging the empty basket. She felt good.

'Morning,' she said brightly going into Bette's office.

'Ah, good. All done?'

'Quite a light post this morning.' She put the basket down on Angela's empty desk.

'She won't be in.' Bette nodded at the desk. 'She phoned earlier. I'm a bit behind actually. You can get the Conference Room ready for the meeting, notebooks, all that. There'll be seven of us. I'd like you to attend, the practice will do your shorthand good.' She fidgeted some papers round her desk.

'Me? At the meeting?'

'Nothing to worry over, just take notes.'

'Take the minutes?' she said stupidly. 'What time is the meeting?'

'Nine-fifteen.' Bette stopped moving the papers and smiled. 'Be good experience. I don't know what form the meeting will take but I gather it's not going to be a full one, so don't worry. I know I can rely on you.'

Sally went to the door.

'Mr Broughton hasn't arrived yet, nor Alan.'

'They'll be here.' Bette was distracted. Sally noticed an uncharacteristic tension about her. She closed the door.

8.40 am

She ran her fingers across the deep shine of the mahogany conference table. Each of the seven places was laid with a fresh white note pad, pencils and pens. She counted them yet again and smiled at her silliness.

138

The week had been one of endings and beginnings and now, for the first time since she started work, she was thinking of her job as a career.

With one final glance over her shoulder, she left the room.

He woke, feeling strange, at least, he thought he had woken. He sat up and looked around, the now familiar scene stretched out below. He felt weak and desperately tired but the silence and the tranquility were soothing. He tried to brush the sleep from his eyes then drew up his knees to his chest and sat, hugging them as he gazed out over the plain.

'Nice to be talking to you in daylight for a change,' said the voice in his head. 'You did well, getting us up here.' There was a long silence.

'I don't understand,' he said aloud.

'That's only because it's too easy,' came the reply. 'You'll be able to see now; it's easier from here.'

'I feel so ... empty.'

'You're no emptier now than you were before; it's just that now you're aware of it, now you have stopped. Watch, you will see.'

But there was nothing to see. The forest to the South was as tangled as ever. The quiet was broken when he heard the riders coming. They broke clear, passing by the hill top.

'Those are tomorrows,' said the voice.

'Tomorrow's what?'

'Just tomorrows. You can spend a lifetime chasing after them but they'll only ever come in their own time, one by one.'

He nodded, understanding, the horseman in the West – he must be today. The scene ran again across his memory. The horse going lame, falling back from the North then veering out to take up station in the West. Tomorrow becoming Today. And the horse it replaces, lame but now too lame to keep up, passing into Yesterday. So, the Southern band were the past.

He sighed thoughtfully. The distance between them is fixed, regardless of speed, no matter how hard you run at tomorrow or how fast you take today.

The hunted feeling, he thought, comes from the pace set. More speed and still more seems to be the solution until that pace is what is expected. Others use it, rely on it and you can't slow down, because there is the scramble to get ahead. Everything disintegrates, there

139

is nothing else, no one else, except you and the running. And the lonelier you are, the better the feeling that you're out in front, clear of the rest. There is only the running left and eventually you have to fall.

There were sounds coming from the forest. But the rider from the East? Again the scene ran out across his memory. Jim, down on the ground with the last of life in him and no tomorrows ahead of him. The horsemen had gathered round – all his days. The big black horse, its skittish dance rippling through the others. Who? The sounds were growing, silence splintering into shards.

'Who knows?' said the voice. 'I am the rider of the black horse – some say – others call him Fate. No one knows. Destiny rides a nervous horse.'

And the noise roared out across the plain. He watched, fascinated, frozen as they came. Hundreds, thousands, millions of them spilling out of the forest. The Runners. The noise was deafening as they came and they came – the population of the world.

He was horrified as they punched and kicked and scratched at one another in their dreadful urge to get ahead, trampling down any unlucky enough to fall. They all avoided the hill. The population of the Earth moving over the Earth in one frantic, headlong rush.

The noise had automatically tensed him up. The sound was in to him, urging him to join them.

'Why do they run?'

'Because they must. But look more closely.'

Some were running easily, free of the scramble, running through their own time, at their own speed.

'And you must run, everyone must – but it doesn't have to be into the ground, not while there are riders still ahead. You may go now: it is time, your time.'

He stood up then ran down the hill to join the rest. At first driven to pick up his old speed then dropping into an easy stride. He glanced over his shoulder and saw a horseman silhouetted on the hill top, then it faded and he ran on.

He woke up, staring at his watch. He was late.

9.15 am

Alan strolled into the Conference Room. He nodded a 'good morning' around the table and sat next to Bette. He gave Sally a brief, approving smile. She returned it, somehow feeling less nervous now he was here. Edgar Broughton still hadn't arrived nor Brian Mann. There was no conversation. Sally sat slightly away from the table, watching them.

They all seemed tired and a little nervous perhaps, even Neil. He was reading through a file of papers. Alan sat opposite him; he had tossed his folder on to the table carelessly and had begun to doodle on the note pad. Next to him, Bette looked at her watch anxiously.

'I wonder what's keeping him?' she said.

David looked at his watch and shrugged.

'Briefing Edgar before his appointment, I should think.' Neil's tone was strained. Sally thought she could detect a note of bitterness and resentment. She felt awkward, out of place and wished Brian Mann would hurry up.

Alan looked across at Neil thoughtfully then returned to his doodling. The door opened and Brian entered.

'Good morning.' He was smiling broadly. 'I'm afraid we have another crisis on our hands,' he said, sitting at the head of the table. 'However, I'll come to that in a moment. This won't take long. First of all, for reasons which will become apparent, I'm proposing that our usual meeting be postponed. I'll reschedule a time later on...'

He paused. Sally was grateful; she had been trying to capture his words verbatim and was losing the battle.

'As you all know,' he said more slowly, 'my absence from this company has increased the burden on you all, not least Bette, and it has been fairly obvious to you that an appointment would be forthcoming. I have worked out a plan which I'd like to outline to you. It has been approved by the board and will take effect in the New Year. No need to take notes, er, Sally, a bulletin will be issued about the management changes.'

Sally stopped, smiling awkwardly and wondered if he was about to ask her to leave but he continued. Everyone turned their gaze back towards him as he spoke.

'You've all responded magnificently to the current crisis, which, I'm confident, is just about beaten thanks to the efforts of Alan and

David here. I understand we should be clear by early Saturday morning?'

David nodded and Alan said, 'Barring major breakdowns, we'll be safe sometime Friday, before lunch, hopefully.'

'That should be enough time for me, I would think,' David said nodding again.

Neil closed his file, impatiently.

'Excellent,' said Brian, shooting Neil a hard side-long glance. 'Our visitors yesterday were most impressed with our methods and so they should be. You will both have important roles to play in the coming months. The board recognizes your contributions to our much improved efficiency and, it is hoped, your expertise will be put to good use over at our other factory. The board have accepted by unreserved recommendation that Bette is to be appointed Managing Director, designate, here. A position, I'm happy to say, she has accepted.'

Sally dropped her notepad in excitement.

Alan threw down his pen, grinning broadly. 'Congratulations!' he said. He put his arm round Bette and kissed her on the cheek.

David's reaction struck Sally as being one of surprise and relief. He stood up and, reaching across the table, shook her hand. Beneath the sudden explosion of congratulations and smiles, Sally caught a terse 'Well done,' from Neil as she retrieved her pad.

Things quietened down. Bette was smiling modestly but with obvious delight.

'She is, of course, eminently qualified and experienced for this position—' Brian was saying, looking at Neil, '—and I'm sure you will give her all the help and support she needs in this difficult task. I will be joining the board at HQ but with special responsibility for our two companies.'

Alan was still smiling as he returned to his doodling.

'Now, sadly, I'm afraid I have the much less pleasant task of announcing that Edgar Broughton is no longer with us. I had a call from his sister shortly before this meeting. He died sometime during the night.'

They all seemed to draw breath at once. Brian's tone had become very solemn yet the words didn't exactly match his manner. Sally recalled his smile when he came in. Her excitement at Bette's appointment was flattened but there was no shock inside her only a mixed up kind of sadness. She looked at the empty chair and

142

wondered why it had to be announced in that way. Somehow it didn't seem right, then she remembered Bette's words only the day before. 'Nothing stops, the world just goes right on over you....'

She looked at Bette, now grim and determined. Alan's jaw was set tight.

'It's not absolutely clear yet what the cause was but his sister said the doctor's first reaction was that it may have been a blood clot. There will, of course, be a post-mortem. Now...', the solemnity dropped from his tone, 'in view of this crisis, I would like you, Neil, to take over Edgar's duties for the moment and I'll be discussing things with you later. I think we ought to adjourn now, give ourselves time to digest this news. I will arrange another meeting probably tomorrow afternoon.'

They all got up. Sally waited for them to leave so that she could clear the table, but Bette beckoned her to follow. She made her way to the door.

'Perhaps you'd like to join me for lunch,' Brian was saying to Neil as they filed slowly out.

'Oh Brian, I'll be needing a cheque for the flowers,' Alan said as they went into the corridor.

'Edgar's?' Brian seemed puzzled.

'No, Jim's,' he said sharply.

'Yes, of course. Now, about this McKenzie job...'

'Well done,' David said quietly to Bette. 'Any help, just let me know.'

She smiled. 'Thanks. I'll appreciate that.'

The voices merged with the sound of the machines as they walked down the corridor. Sally followed Bette into the office. She let out a big sigh of relief when the door closed.

'Thank God that's over. Promise you one thing, Sally, you won't attend many meetings like that one, but you will attend many more, I'm sure.'

They sat down.

'It's marvellous, I'm very happy for you. Did you know – about Edgar, I mean?'

'No. Brian sprung that on us all. Hardly seems possible, does it?'

Without knowing why, Sally was glad she hadn't known.

'I'd better draft an advert for my replacement,' she said. 'Meant to do that on Monday. Don't worry, it'll be someone we can all get on with and hopefully, later on, you'll be working more with me as my Assistant.'

Sally laughed.

'That would be great.'

'Hectic is more the word, still, we'll see. Right. Leave the Conference Room for the time being, clear that up later. I think you ought to see if there's been a second delivery yet, get that sorted, so if there are any stray orders they can be processed immediately.'

10.05 am

Sally had just taken a handful of envelopes to the Order Department and there were a few for delivery along the corridor.

David Myers was on the telephone apparently waiting for some information. He tapped his fingers on the desk. She put his mail down in front of him; he smiled warmly and nodded.

'Yes, fire away,' he said, picking up his pen.

Neil Telford was reading the morning paper. It was spread over his desk. She put his letters on the corner and noticed he was studying the Appointments page. He looked up, startled, as if he had been unaware of her presence and turned the page.

Alan was on the telephone; she could hear the noise of the machines coming from the earpiece, the sound familiar but smaller, reduced to fit the size of the phone.

'Bob? How far are you with this McKenzie thing?' He winked at her as she handed him the mail. He looked tired.

Edgar Broughton's office was cold and empty. She put some letters on his desk and left as gratefully as ever.

In Bette's office, she handed her some post and said, 'I'll tidy the Conference Room now, shall I?'

Bette nodded.

10.15 am

She looked out at the falling snow from the window in the Conference Room. She couldn't help feeling that she ought to be more saddened by Edgar's death but she wasn't and no one else seemed very upset. Jim had stopped the factory but – nothing really stops it, she reflected, turning away from the window, nothing can even slow it down, not for a moment.

She began to collect up the notepads, pausing at Alan's to see what he had drawn. She tore off the page and folded it carefully.

Outside, in the corridor, she was greeted by the roaring, stamping noise of the printing machines down below. She watched them a moment and the bustling movement on the shop floor. The machines turned out the bright and happy Christmas cards endlessly. Merry Christmas, they said, once, twice, a thousand times over. Merry Christmas. It all seemed suddenly misplaced.

She unfolded the page again and stared at it bemused, a horseman drawn in silhouette.